The Trudie Fine
Mystery Series

A Fine Fix
Fine Dining
Fine Arts

Fine Arts

A Trudie Fine Mystery
By
Gale Deitch

Rosedale Press

Fine Arts
First Edition
Copyright©2016 by Gale Deitch

Rosedale Press Trade Paperback
ISBN-13: 978-1540372253
ISBN-10: 1540372251
www.gdeitchblog.com

Cover Design: www.earthlycharms.com
Author's Photo: Holly Callen Berardi

To Marcie and Matt

I think every woman should have a blowtorch.

Julia Child

Chapter One

Even better than doing what you love most is getting to do it with your best friend. It's like sprinkling sesame seeds over peanut noodles or rippling caramel sauce through vanilla ice cream. And, as Zach and I arranged assortments of canapés on silver platters, nothing made us happier than working side-by-side to create delicious food to delight our customers and their guests.

Zachary Cohen and I had been best friends since childhood and were currently co-owners of a busy catering company, *A Fine Fix*. For tonight's art show opening, we had prepared delicacies like endive with herbed cheese and smoked salmon, wasabi shrimp, mushroom tartlets, and miniature beef wellingtons. Armed with our goodies, we stepped out of the small kitchenette and into the main gallery area where guests milled around surveying the works on display at the privately owned Christine Dugan Gallery in Dupont Circle, only blocks from the White House.

Jennifer Hall, the owner of a coffee shop who supplied us with her scrumptious cakes and breads, headed toward us, a friend in tow. "There they are," she said. The woman with her was tall and slender, one of those delicate-boned natural beauties who could slip into a dress and heels, run her fingers through her short, wavy hair and *voila*, she was ready.

Jennifer grinned. "Trudie, Zach, meet the woman of the hour, my partner, Rose Mendez."

Partner? In the few months I'd known Jennifer, I realized I knew very little about her personal life, but it was clear she wasn't referring to a business partner.

I set my platter down on a small table and held out my hand to Rose. "Trudie Fine." I gestured to Zach. "And this is *my* partner, Zachary Cohen. Well, co-owner of our catering company."

Rose shook our hands. "Thank you so much for catering tonight. This is my first showing, and I'm a little nervous about putting my work out for the world to see." She glanced at our trays. "It looks like you're adding some class to the evening."

"Thanks. We're happy to do it." The spark in Zach's eyes acknowledged this lovely young woman in front of him. She had full, pouty lips with just a touch of natural-colored lip gloss, apparently the only bit of makeup she needed. It was difficult even for me to take my eyes off Rose with her short black hair, large chocolate eyes framed with dark lashes, and sharply defined cheek bones.

Rose glanced at Jennifer. "I guess we'd better get back to mingling with our guests." As they turned to join the others, Rose took Jennifer's hand, leaned over and kissed her on the lips.

Zach and I looked at each other, everything becoming clear as the bell on a kitchen timer, and I emitted a quiet snort of laughter.

Definitely not Jennifer's business partner.

The two of us strolled in different directions, weaving through the gathering, platters of *hors d'oeuvres* in hand. Gordon, the server we had hired for the evening, did the same with his tray of glasses of red and white wine. The pimply young man wore a black suit and a purple bow tie we had loaned him for the evening, which coordinated with our company's color theme. Zach was dressed in a black shirt and pants and purple silk tie, while I wore my purple apron with our logo embroidered in orange across the breast pocket.

As I offered canapés, I took a peek at some of Rose's art work. The framed pieces on the walls were huge, and I had to look up at them from my five-foot-two frame. Acrylics of grays and blacks slashed across stark white canvas, each with only a single color weaving through. The metal sculptures, about seven or eight feet tall and set randomly around the room, imitated the wall art, but in three dimensions. I wondered how the lovely, delicate woman I had just met could create such bold statements in her artwork.

Classical music played softly in the background as guests wandered through the gallery, surveying Rose's work. A placard by each piece displayed titles like *In the Womb*, which featured a stream of yellow spiraling to the top, and *Last Breath*, a series of ascending steps that gradually faded to light gray where it emitted a stream of blue. I realized that the sequence of the art show indicated an entire life span but couldn't really discern how each title related to the piece in front of me. I wouldn't have been able to tell which was which if someone had scrambled the placards and placed them randomly.

3

The clinking of a spoon against a wine glass drew everyone's attention to a woman who stood in the center of the gallery, her stark white-blonde, shoulder-length hair straight as uncooked spaghetti. A red metal pendant sat low and heavy on her flat chest, and spiraled to a long, sharp point against her black and white dress, causing her to resemble one of Rose's sculptures.

"Ladies and gentlemen," she said when everyone had turned to her. "I am Christine Dugan and I'd like to thank you for coming tonight to view the work of what could be the most important artist of the decade, Rose Mendez." Guests applauded as she extended a hand toward Rose, who approached, hugged Christine and stood beside her, smiling modestly.

"Feast your eyes on this remarkable work," Christine continued, gesturing toward the paintings and sculptures around the room. "You may never get the chance to see anything like this again all together in one place. For now, let's toast this exceptional artist and enjoy the evening. And please, if you have any questions or are interested in a purchase, feel free to speak to me or one of my assistants, Amy or Rick." Christine nodded to her left toward Amy, a mousy, young woman in a boxy dress and clunky black pumps. Rick stood confidently beside her in a charcoal suit that accentuated his wide shoulders and slim waist. His tanned, chiseled features and dimpled smile caused me to flush as if I'd just lifted the lid on a simmering stew.

Amy had been the one I'd dealt with to arrange the catering. She had been a little cool to deal with, as the gallery had its own preferred caterers. But Rose had requested our services tonight, on Jennifer's recommendation, and they'd grudgingly accepted. Zach and I had followed all their strict rules about timing, parking, and serving, and once Amy had sampled our fare, she'd warmed up to us and actually said she would add us to their catering list.

On one of my trips to the kitchen, I spotted Rose and Christine having what looked like a heated discussion in a corner behind one of her sculptures. Rose was frowning and shaking her head. I imagined they had business to discuss, but what kind of business, I didn't know and didn't want to know. As I passed, I overheard Rose hiss, "I thought I'd made it clear that I'd be getting sixty percent. That's the going rate at any gallery."

"Rose dear," Christine murmured in a calming voice. "You signed the agreement. It was all spelled out in black and white. I think fifty-fifty is quite fair. These days my competitors down the street are taking sixty."

Emerging from the kitchen again with another tray of *hors d'oeurves*, I noticed the two of them still deep in conversation. They must have resolved their differences because they now seemed to be engaged in some sort of intimate banter as Rose fiddled with the chain around Christine's neck and adjusted the tilt of the metal pendant against her chest. I couldn't imagine wearing a necklace like that with its double helix spiraling down about seven or eight inches and ending in a sharp, menacing point.

Shouts from the front hall caused me, and others, to turn.

"It's not fair," a woman yelled as she plodded across the gallery floor, her disheveled hair flying. "Not fair, Christine. I was on the schedule for this showing, not her. It was my turn and you bumped me." Her eyes narrowed as she approached them and, with both hands, she shoved Christine backwards against the wall.

The heavy red pendant bounced against Christine's chest.

Gasps and murmurs buzzed through the room as Rick rushed over and grabbed onto the woman's arm. "Deanna," he said. "This isn't the time or the place."

She wrenched herself free and folded her arms around her shapeless gray sweater, breathing hard. "Oh, yes. This is the perfect time and place," she said, looking from guest to guest. "This showing was supposed to be mine, not hers. Don't you see? You're supposed to be looking at my work. My work," she shouted.

Everyone stood in silence watching this woman who, with her untamed graying mane and fingers stained with blue and green pastel paints, had apparently thrown on her sweater over a cotton peasant blouse and a faded, batik-print skirt and headed to the gallery without a thought about her appearance or the chilly mid-November temperature outside.

I was as shocked as anyone by her actions, but I also could understand her indignation if, in fact, she had been bumped from the show schedule. I wondered if Christine had made the decision based on the quality of the woman's art or, more likely, on a relationship that had soured.

Rick approached the woman again and gently put his hands on her shoulders. "It's okay, Deanna. Everything's okay."

"No, it's not okay." She shook her head and stamped a sandaled foot on the hardwood floor. "I'm not leaving until she puts me back on the schedule."

Christine lifted her chin. "Deanna, you need to stop this childish behavior. Now go on home and call me in the morning. We'll talk then."

"And you'll put me back on the schedule?"

"I have an opening coming up. We'll discuss it in the morning. Rick, please escort Deanna to the door."

Rick bent down to murmur in her ear. "Let's get you home, all right?"

Her expression softened, and she turned and peered up at Rick, nodding.

"Amy," he said, walking Deanna toward the front hall. "Please call for a taxi."

Christine smoothed her dress and patted her hair, then smiled. "Ladies and gentlemen. I apologize for the disruption. Please enjoy the rest of the evening."

Over the next half hour, as smatterings of conversation ebbed and flowed through the gallery, we continued passing our canapés and retrieving dirty napkins and plates. Then Zach wheeled in a round table set with an assortment of mini pastries Jennifer had prepared, like delicate pink and green petit fours, multi-layered Napoleons and colorful little fruit tarts. We had arranged pedestals at varying heights so that the platters of desserts sat at different levels and could be reached from any side of the table.

The evening was winding down, and I grinned at the thought of getting off my feet and snuggling under the covers with Daniel. Detective Daniel Goldman and I had been together for about four months. He was the first man who actually loved me just the way I was—short, plump body and all.

While guests enjoyed dessert, I brought a couple of empty trays into the kitchenette then headed down the narrow hall to the ladies' room. Loud voices emerging from behind a closed door caught my attention, and I stopped to listen.

"But Aunt Christine, that stuff is unsellable," I heard Amy say.

"No more excuses. I don't care what kind of crap is on display in our gallery. When you're speaking to our customers, it's the most important work that's come along. I can't afford to float both of you, so if you want to keep your jobs, get out there and sell at least two pieces each tonight. Otherwise, one of you has to go."

"Two pieces each?" Amy said. "Of those monstrosities?"

I didn't know much about contemporary art, but I thought Rose's work was striking and could work well in the right place. I did wonder, however, how much her art sold for and where in a home someone would place something so huge.

"Stop complaining and just do it," Christine said. "And get someone to bring me another glass of wine."

The door opened, so I ducked into the darkness of an alcove and held my breath.

"One person has to go all right," Rick mumbled under his breath as he and Amy passed me on their way toward the gallery. "But it's not you or me."

I waited until the clack of Amy's pumps receded. Then I exhaled a sigh of relief and continued down the hall past Christine's closed-door office to the ladies' room.

When I returned to the main room, I spotted Amy and Rick busy speaking with guests, working hard to get some sales. Rick seemed to be targeting the women in the room, and by the way he easily engaged their attention with a smile or a touch, I guessed he would have more success than Amy.

As our server passed with his tray, collecting empty glasses and dirty plates, I stopped him. "Gordon, why don't you make one more round with the wine to see who might like a refill?" Then I remembered Christine's request. "Oh, and bring some wine to Ms. Dugan, the director. She's in her office."

"Sure," he said with a nonchalant shrug and headed for the kitchen, making me feel like a mother who'd just asked her teenage son to take out the trash. I knew he had to be at least eighteen to work for the agency as a server, but this kid didn't even look old enough to drive.

Jennifer approached and took me aside. "See that man speaking with Rose?" She nodded in their direction. "He's the art critic from *The Washington Post*. Trudie, this is her big chance to be recognized nationally. I'm just so proud of her."

I glanced across the gallery. Rose stood quite close to a middle-aged man with a dark goatee and a bit of a belly. She put her hand on his arm, and he leaned toward her and whispered in her ear, causing her to giggle and redden.

Thinking about the scene I'd observed earlier between Rose and

Christine, I turned to Jennifer to see her reaction to this intimate encounter right in the middle of the gallery floor.

"It's just an act, Trudie," Jennifer said, noticing my expression. "Getting media attention is a constant struggle for an artist. So if a little bit of flirting helps, that's what she's going to do."

Since I'd met Jennifer Hall, I'd admired her strength and resilience in owning and operating her own coffee shop on U Street. Barely thirty like me, her confident demeanor made this petite woman with the pixie haircut seem older than her years. But I wondered if she might be burying her head in the sand, choosing not to notice her partner's actions.

"How long have you and Rose been together?" I asked.

"Since last summer. Don't you remember? I brought her to the grand re-opening at *Maybelline's*." She smiled. "That was actually our first date."

"Oh, yeah." I vaguely remembered Jennifer having dinner with a woman at my friend May's restaurant, but I hadn't paid much attention to them. I couldn't even remember if we'd been introduced. At the time, I'd been trying to recover from some harrowing attempts on my life, and it had all become one big blur.

Jennifer still didn't seem fazed by her partner's encounter with the critic, even though the blatant flirting continued. "Rose moved in with me in September. She's been using the barn behind my house as her studio. Isn't it amazing what she's produced?"

"I should say so," I said, scanning the works around the room. "I can't even imagine how she can construct such huge sculptures."

Jennifer laughed. "I know. Hard to believe. She has a knack with ladders and welding irons. You ought to come by some time to watch her work."

Zach emerged from the kitchen and joined the two of us. "Your pastries are a big hit, as usual," he said to Jennifer. "I hope there'll be a few left over to snack on later."

"If not, I'll have some for you in the morning when you help me with that wedding cake."

Jennifer had been teaching Zach the art of decorating wedding cakes, and he'd gotten pretty good at it. The cake for the wedding we'd be catering on Saturday would be particularly intricate with its lacey patterns on the icing and fondant bows.

"I'll be there bright and early," he said. "Be sure to get the coffee brewing."

"Uh, I run a coffee shop, remember? That would be the first thing I do every morning."

The three of us turned to a clattering of loud footsteps on the polished hardwood. Gordon came barreling into the gallery, wild-eyed, his tray of wine bottles and glasses crashing to the floor. His face was pale as a vanilla-iced cupcake.

He looked directly at me and pointed behind him. "Sh-she's d-dead!" he blurted out.

For a moment, we all just looked at Gordon, uncomprehending, as the mess of shattered glass and red and white wine pooled, rivulets spreading toward the hallway like fingers pointing the way. Then Rick sprinted out of the gallery to the back hall with Amy at his heels and others following.

Zach gestured for me to stay put and headed toward the commotion. I followed him anyway, gingerly side-stepping the glass shards and growing puddle of wine, which now, as the red and white liquid swirled together, resembled a pink Zinfandel.

Too many people crowded the hallway outside Christine's office. Shrieks and moans emerged from the room, and the *Post* art critic fled toward the men's room, his hand covering his mouth.

Zach pushed his way through with me close behind. At the doorway, he stopped short. At six-foot-two, he could easily see above the heads of others. I wedged myself in beside him and gasped at the sight.

Christine Dugan, at first glance, appeared to be reclining comfortably in her chair—until I realized she'd been impaled through the heart with her own red, metal pendant, a trail of blood weaving down through the folds of her dress, her unseeing eyes open wide.

Chapter Two

Loud sirens announced the arrival of the police. They entered through the gallery, a few heading toward Christine's office while others directed guests and staff to remain for questioning.

People stood in small clusters, some speaking in hushed whispers, others crying. I heard someone sobbing and turned to see Rick seated with his arm around Amy, her eyes red and her cheeks streaked with tears. In another corner, Jennifer and Rose stood side-by-side, holding each other quietly.

Zach and I took the responsibility of trying to keep people calm, and once Gordon had recovered from his gruesome discovery, we kept him busy filling pitchers of ice water and serving it to frantic guests until a detective pulled him aside to interrogate him. After all, Gordon was the one to discover the body. Shoulders drooping, he handed the tray of ice water to me.

"Don't worry," I said to him. "Just answer his questions honestly and you'll be okay."

He shot me a doubtful look and followed the detective to one of the offices in the back hallway.

A short, stocky man with a bald head and lots of dark facial hair rushed into the gallery, his rubber-soled shoes squeaking as he made his way across the gallery floor. I recognized him as the same medical examiner that had been called to *Maybelline's* last summer in a different investigation. I wondered how many MEs were on the payroll of the Metropolitan Police Department.

The clinking of ice cubes in the glasses on my tray caught my attention, and I realized my hands were trembling like an out-of-control blender. Zach took the tray from me and set it down on a table, then walked me over to a chair. "Trudie, you're upset. Sit down and relax. I'll serve the water."

I peered up at him and nodded, unable to protest or even answer, as if my vocal cords had been sitting in the freezer and still hadn't thawed. I couldn't stop myself from shaking and hugged my body tightly. I'd seen dead bodies before. I should be used to it by now. But how does anyone ever get used to something like this? One moment, Christine was the vibrant life force of this gallery, and the next, she was gone.

I stared into space, desiring only to be home, buried under the covers, far away from this place. I wondered how I would survive the evening.

Daniel. I had to call him. I needed him.

I pulled my cellphone from my apron pocket, but before I could even call, there across the room was Daniel heading straight for me.

"Trudie," he said, pulling me to my feet and wrapping his arms around me. "Are you okay? As soon as I heard the report on the police radio, I rushed over."

The relief of being enveloped in Daniel's arms overwhelmed me. I looked up at him, my eyes beginning to stream. "I'm fine," I said. "Now that you're here." I nuzzled my head against his chest and basked in the solid warmth of his body.

"Detective Goldman." A uniformed officer approached. "Glad you made it. With all the demonstrators over at the Supreme Court building and another fence-jumper at the White House, we're a little short-handed tonight."

I held on tighter to Daniel, not wanting him to leave.

"Sure. Give me a minute," he said to the officer, who nodded and walked away.

Daniel put his hand under my chin and lifted until I was looking up into his deep, golden eyes. He brushed my hair out of my face and put his warm hand on my cheek. "I'll be right here, Trudie. Just hang on while I help with the investigation. When we're finished, I'll take you home. Okay?"

I nodded. What else was there to do but wait?

One by one, guests who'd been interrogated were released, and the gallery began to empty so that Zach's approaching footsteps on the hardwood floor echoed through the room. He knelt down beside my chair and put his hand on my shoulder. "Gordon helped me clean up and load the van, so why don't I take it back to the warehouse?" he said. "You go home with Daniel and get some sleep."

"Thanks, Zach. I'll help unload the van in the morning."

"Don't worry about it, Trudie. Take the morning off. Remember, I'll be starting the day at Jennifer's coffee shop. Okay?"

I nodded and watched Zach head back into the kitchen. Sitting alone in the gallery, now devoid of people, I began to tremble. Rose's cold, industrial sculptures sent chills down my spine. Meant to depict the human life span, to me they represented anything but that. In fact, they only brought to mind the image of Christine's lifeless eyes as she lay dead in her office.

"Trudie."

Daniel's voice startled me, and I jumped.

"They're ready for you now," he said.

"Ready for what?"

"For questioning, baby. You're the last one. Then I promise we'll go home."

It hadn't occurred to me that I'd be questioned, too. But of course that made sense. Daniel took my hand and led me to a small office in the back hallway.

"I'll wait out here for you."

"You're not coming in?" I asked, swallowing back my disappointment.

"Can't. Not allowed. You'll do fine." He nodded me toward the door.

My legs felt shaky as I entered the room. The uniformed officer stood stiffly behind the desk and gestured for me to sit in a chair across from him. He seemed young for this job, a typical rookie with close-cropped dark hair and a serious demeanor. Even after I sat, he continued to stand and got right down to business, handing me his card which read, "Officer William Billings, Third District Station, Metropolitan Police Department." I wondered if people called him Bill Billings.

"Normally, Detective Goldman would handle all the interrogations," he said, pacing back and forth behind his chair. "But because of your personal relationship with him, and since I am assisting him in this investigation, I will be conducting this interview with you."

He stopped and regarded me, his hands resting on the back of his chair. "Let me inform you, Miss Fine that I am recording this conversation to ensure I get accurate information."

"Okay."

"Please state your name and address for the record."

"Trudie Fine," I said then paused.

Uh, oh, I thought. My address should be the easiest question he asked. But my official address was my condo, which I hadn't been able to sell after months on the market. I couldn't live in it either since the harrowing experience I'd been through last summer. I could give my parents' address, where I occasionally stayed the night. But truthfully, I was living at Daniel's house almost full time, so that was the address I decided to give.

"And your place of work?"

"*A Fine Fix*, my catering company on Nebel Street in Rockville." This I spouted out easily, happy to share with anyone who'd listen. A business woman had to take every opportunity to market herself.

He looked at me. "And I understand you were catering tonight's event, correct?"

"Yes, I was."

Officer Billings began pacing again, his hands linked behind his back, his face all chiseled, sharp angles. I noticed dark shadows under his eyes, and a clenched jaw. His uniform had been crisply pressed. I knew that if I'd been able to see his shoes they would be polished to a mirror finish.

I smiled, thinking of the first time I'd met Daniel at another crime scene. His interrogation had been so much different with his relaxed demeanor and well-worn navy blazer and khakis as he sat in a comfortable living room chair taking notes with a pencil and pad. His laid-back approach put people at ease and probably helped them relax and open up.

Officer Billings stopped pacing and turned to me. "Tell me, Miss Fine, anything you may have seen or heard this evening that was out of the ordinary."

I wished he would sit down so I wouldn't have to keep craning my neck to look up at him. The glare from the ceiling lights caused my eyes to water.

"Well, that art work in the gallery is certainly out of the ordinary, isn't it?" I snorted a laugh.

"Miss Fine, a murder has been committed tonight and it is no laughing matter." He glared at me.

"Yes, sir," was all I could manage with this guy. Exhaustion, both physical and emotional, was working its way into my body, and I felt like the churning motor of my old mixer just before it decided to die. My lower lip began to tremble, and I bit it hard to keep from crying.

Bill Billings must have noticed my distress because his gaze softened. He sat down at the desk and began again. "I'm sorry, Miss Fine. I realize it's been a long evening. I just have a couple of questions and then you're free to leave. All right?"

I nodded, but I wished he would stop calling me "Miss Fine."

"Now is there anything you saw or overheard tonight that might be significant in our investigation?"

I thought a moment. "Yes. Christine and Rose. They were arguing about the percentage of sales the gallery would take. Rose was pretty angry, but Christine said it was all spelled out in the signed contract."

He sat up straighter as if I'd gotten his attention. "And?"

"And that's when that woman barged into the gallery. I'm sure others have told you about her. Deanna, I think her name was." I described the disgruntled artist disturbed with Christine. "She even got physical and pushed her into the wall. But they escorted her out, called a taxi to take her home."

"Yes, I heard about that incident from others."

Officer Billings' cell phone rang. "One moment." He stood and turned his back to me.

As I waited for him to finish his call, I surveyed the room. From the few feminine touches, a tape dispenser shaped like a high-heeled shoe and a glass dish filled with pink paper clips, I assumed this was Amy's office. Sure enough, photos on the shelves included a graduation picture of Amy flanked by a man and woman, probably her parents. Another showed her sitting at a restaurant or club with a girlfriend, both tanned and smiling, two enormous tropical drinks in front of them. Spring break in Cancun, maybe?

"I'm sorry, Miss Fine. I have to cut this short and get back to the station." He pressed the *off* button on his recorder and picked it up, a signal that the interrogation was over.

Cut this short? I hadn't even told him what I'd overheard outside Christine's door when she was lecturing her two assistants, threatening termination if they didn't make some sales tonight. Or about Rick's murmured comment as he left her office.

"But—"

The officer exhaled his impatience. "You're free to go now. If you think of anything else, call me. You have my card."

Well, if he didn't want to hear anything else I had to offer then I wasn't going to worry about it. Officially dismissed, I rose to leave, checking my watch. Eleven-thirty already. After a long evening, I'd been the last person questioned but thought Bill Billings had a lot to learn about manners.

I glanced across the desk at him. "You're welcome," I said.

"What?"

"You're welcome. You say, 'thank you,' then I say, 'you're welcome.'" I folded my arms and waited, looking him right in the eye.

He reddened. "Thank you, Miss Fine."

"You're welcome."

Chapter Three

I woke to the smell of fresh coffee and checked my cell phone for the time. Eight o'clock. It felt nice to sleep a little later. Wondering if Daniel had left for work yet, I padded out to the kitchen and found him at the sink, rinsing out his cereal bowl.

"Hey," I said.

He glanced at me and grinned. "Hey yourself, beautiful. Sleep well?"

After all this time with Daniel, I still wasn't sure what he saw in me that appealed to him. Especially first thing in the morning as I stood there wearing his old flannel shirt that I loved to sleep in, my feet bare, my hair disheveled, and not a stitch of makeup.

"Like a cheese log. I needed it." I thought about the night before, and Christine's dead body came to mind. I shivered.

"Oh, baby," Daniel dried his hands on a dish towel and walked over to me. "It was a rough one for you, wasn't it?" He brushed the hair out of my face with his fingers then kissed me softly on the lips.

It felt good, but I stepped back. "Do you really want to do that? I haven't brushed my teeth yet."

He laughed and closed in for another kiss, his arms warm and comforting. "Wish I didn't have to get to work. Will you be okay? What are you doing today?"

"I'll be fine. I'm meeting Zach at the office later this afternoon to wrap up last night's event, get everything put away. Then we're heading over to Ally's restaurant to give her a hand. Remember her soft opening is tonight. Will you be there?"

"Sure. Wouldn't miss it. What is a soft opening anyway?" He took my hand and led me toward the front hall.

"It's a kind of practice night. Ally's invited her family, friends and business contacts for a free dinner. It's a good way for new restaurants to test out the menu, the staff and service. I think she's going to have a couple of these before the big grand opening."

He retrieved his leather jacket from the coat tree in the foyer then pulled me in for a kiss with his free arm. "So we're going to be her guinea pigs tonight, huh?"

"Don't knock it," I said, standing on tip toes to kiss him back. "It's a free meal."

After Daniel left, I showered and dressed, enjoying the leisurely pace of not having to be anywhere yet. My serenity was interrupted by my ringing phone.

"Hi, Trudie," Zach said. "Hope I didn't wake you."

"No. I'm already dressed and wondering what to do next. I'm not used to having the whole morning to myself. What's up?"

"I'm at the coffee shop with Jennifer. We're decorating the

wedding cake. She was wondering if you could do her a big favor and pick up a sketch she left at her house."

"A sketch of what?" I asked. "And how am I going to get into her house?"

"The bride called her yesterday with an idea for an alternate design on the cake. So Jennifer sketched it out but left it on her kitchen counter and forgot to bring it to work this morning. Rose is working on a project in the barn, and Jennifer can't reach her. Just go out back to the barn and Rose will let you in the house."

The thought of seeing more of Rose's art pieces freaked me out a little. It would bring all the events of the night before into clear focus. I wasn't sure I was ready for that. But the sketch Jennifer needed was for the wedding we were catering this weekend, so of course I would get it. And I had been interested in watching Rose work on her sculptures.

"Okay. I'll leave now."

I'd only been to Jennifer's house once to drop off a check, so I drove slowly down her street trying to identify the correct house. As soon as I saw it, though, with its blue siding and the grape arbor along the side of the house, I knew that was it. I parked my car at the curb and walked hesitantly through the arbor to the back yard.

The red barn was larger than I'd expected. I'd been imagining something the size of a shed. Instead, this was a massive two-story structure. I wondered why Jennifer would even have wanted something like this when she'd bought the house. Then I remembered her telling me that an uncle had left the house to her when he passed away.

The barn door creaked as I opened it. "Rose?" I called, stepping inside.

A barking dog leaped toward me and I froze.

Standing about five feet from me, the dog growled, his head swiveling from side to side as he examined me. His short-haired coat was white and mottled with gray.

"Sit, Zeus." Rose's laugh came from somewhere up near the rafters. I looked up and spotted her on a tall ladder wearing a protective shield over her eyes.

The dog was sitting now, as commanded.

"Will he...bite me?" I asked, still not moving.

"Zeus?" she said. "Never. He loves people. You just startled him. That's all."

I looked back at the dog, who danced on his front paws, anxious to approach me. His ears pointed upward and he panted with excitement, his tongue hanging out the side of his mouth. I knelt down and held out my hand to him. "Well hi, Zeus. Happy to meet you."

He whined and peered up at Rose who laughed again and signaled to him with her hand. "Okay. Go ahead."

As Zeus approached me, his tail wagged wildly. He sniffed my fingers and looked up at me with dark, moist eyes.

"You're a sweetheart," I said. As I ran my hand over his smooth, warm coat, his ears went back. "I think we've just become friends, Zeus."

"I think you have," Rose said. "Just give me a moment and I'll come down."

I peered up at her. In her gray jumpsuit, heavy gloves and helmet with the flat rectangular window for viewing, Rose could have been an astronaut or a bee keeper. She held a long metal tool I assumed was her welding iron. Bright orange sparks flamed, buzzed and crackled as she ran it along the edge of the sculpture she was working on. Except for the tangy, iron oxide smell that hung in the air, it reminded me of the blow torch I use to caramelize the top layer of crème brûlée.

"That'll do it for now," she said, coming down the ladder and shedding her protective gear onto a work table.

"Sorry to interrupt your work," I said. "Jennifer asked me to come over to pick up something she left in the kitchen."

"Not a problem. I have to get going soon anyway. What does she need?" Rose walked toward me, a wide grin on her face. Even in a pair of faded overalls and scuffed brown work boots, she looked like a model stepping out of the pages of a fashion magazine.

"It's a sketch she made for the wedding cake."

"Oh, yeah. Evidently, the bride called her with some last minute changes. I think I did see her sketch pad on the counter this morning. Come on in." She led the way across the yard to the back door, Zeus keeping pace at her side. The door opened with an easy turn of the knob into the mud room where Rose shed her boots.

"I guess I could have come in and grabbed the sketch pad myself without bothering you if I'd known the door would be unlocked," I said.

Rose smiled and shook her head. "Not really. Zeus would have heard you and barked his head off. Then I would have had to stop in the middle of a crucial welding to find out who or what was in the yard. Believe me, your coming to the barn to get me was definitely the way to go."

I followed her into the kitchen, and sighed with envy at the distressed green cabinets, white marble counter tops, and updated appliances. A long farmhouse table with a mix of chairs in random colors made this room the perfect place to entertain friends.

Rose opened a cabinet and set out a couple of coffee mugs, while Zeus lapped up huge slurps of water from his bowl and then settled himself into his bed in the corner.

"Here it is," Rose said, picking up a sketch pad from the counter and handing it to me.

The pad was opened to a pencil drawing of a wedding cake with an intricate weave design around the alternate layers.

"Nice," I said. "The cake is going to look spectacular."

Rose cocked her head to examine the drawing, exposing her long, slender neck. "Jennifer is a master at wedding cakes. You're lucky to have her working with you."

"You're telling me. I don't know what we would have done without her these past few months. Our business has taken off, and I think her incredible baking skills had a lot to do with that."

Rose looked at her watch. "Listen, Trudie. Zeus and I have agility training at eleven. I need to change my clothes and get going in a few minutes."

Zeus popped his head up at the sound of his name.

"What's agility training?" I asked.

"It's an obstacle course for dogs where they learn to navigate a series of apparatus. Zeus loves it, and it's great exercise for both of us. He's even won some ribbons in competition." She poured the coffee and set out cream and sweeteners. Then she grabbed a large handful of dog biscuits from a glass container on the counter and put all but one of them in a Ziploc bag.

Zeus stood and scrambled over to her.

Rose held up the biscuit and the dog instantly sat, his eyes riveted to the treat. She moved it closer and closer to the dog, and although he seemed to want it badly, he did not move. Rose made an almost imperceptible gesture with her hand, and Zeus took the treat in his mouth and gobbled it up.

"Good boy," Rose said, kneeling to his level and running her hands over his coat playfully.

"Zeus seems to love those dog biscuits," I said.

"He does. Jennifer makes them special for Zeus, and he won't eat any other treat but hers."

"Jennifer makes them?" Intrigued, I walked over to the container of goodies, lifted the lid and took one out to take a whiff. "Smells delicious," I said. "Like a cookie. I wonder what she puts in them. Can I taste it?"

"Sure, they're fit for human consumption. I don't know what she puts in these things, but this dog will do anything for them. I'm bringing a few with us to agility training." Rose glanced up at me.

I nibbled a corner of a biscuit and nodded my head. "Not bad. I can see why Zeus loves them so much. Can I give him the rest of this one?"

"Sure."

I held out the biscuit the way Rose had and Zeus sat obediently waiting. Then I mimicked her hand signal, and the dog approached for his treat.

"Hey, you're pretty good at that," Rose said to me. "A quick learner. Why don't you come with us and watch Zeus at agility training?"

"Me? I don't know. I have to drop off the sketch at the coffee shop all the way down on U Street. There really isn't any time."

"Wait a minute." Rose stood and pulled the sketch pad from my hand. "It's the twenty-first century, remember?" She sat down at the desk in the corner of the kitchen, turned on the computer then scanned and emailed the drawing, and made a quick call to Jennifer to make sure she'd received it.

"*Voila.*" She swiveled her chair around and grinned at me. "I just saved you at least a good hour."

I laughed. "I guess you did."

"Honestly, Jen is still back in the dark ages where technology is concerned. I'm constantly reminding her that there are faster ways to get certain things done." She stood up, and Zeus perked his head up expectantly. "So, you want to come with us, Trudie?"

"Where?"

She rolled her eyes. "To agility training."

Hearing those words, Zeus stood and whined at Rose, dancing on his front paws.

"See," she said to me. "Zeus can't wait. I'm sure he'd love to show off for you."

"Well, I don't have to be anywhere until two this afternoon. Sure. That might be fun to watch."

"I'm just going to run upstairs to change. Help yourself to some more coffee."

While I waited for Rose, I sipped my coffee and wandered into the living room. It was decorated in that shabby chic look I loved with a sturdy coffee table made of distressed pale wood and an overstuffed sofa and side chairs in soft blues, grays and creams.

I stood for a few moments admiring the view out the French doors that led to a lovely walled courtyard with climbing vines, large ceramic planters and wrought iron, cushioned chairs. Then, while heading back to the kitchen, I noticed a huge painting that covered almost an entire wall, definitely Rose's work. This one, however, grabbed my attention more than the others I'd seen at the gallery. It had the same blacks and grays scrawled across the white canvas, but a rainbow of intricate threads wove around and through each other into a beautiful scrollwork design.

"Like it?" Rose asked, startling me.

"Yes, it's amazing."

She smiled. "Probably my favorite piece, too. It represents Jennifer and me, our relationship, our love."

Rose had changed into jeans and a white tank top that clung to her slim body and made it clear she was not wearing a bra.

"Won't you be cold in that?" I asked. "It's chilly out there."

She laughed. "It gets pretty warm running around the agility ring. I'll just grab a jacket."

As we walked back toward the kitchen, I stopped short. Displayed on a shelf were a variety of twisted pieces of colored metal. Examining them, I wondered why they seemed so familiar.

Rose turned and said, "What do you think? I'm trying my hand at metal-sculpted jewelry."

I ran my fingers along the necklaces and bracelets and their various shapes, some folded at irregular angles, others gently curving, until I came to a spiraled piece. I yanked my hand back and inhaled sharply. "Th-that looks like...," I started.

"Yes," Rose said. "It's a duplicate of the one Christine wore last night. I gave to it her to wear at the opening."

The room began to spin, and a chill shot through me as I recalled the necklace hanging heavily from Christine's neck and then later, its sharp spiraled point impaled into her chest.

Chapter Four

Zeus paced across the back seat of Rose's car. Whenever we stopped at a traffic light, he stuck his head between the two of us, panting heated breaths. A few times, I felt his cold nose on my neck.

"How are you doing after last night?" I asked Rose.

She shook her head. "I've been trying not to think about it. I mean, here was my big break to bring my work front and center in the art world. A gallery filled with art collectors and connoisseurs, prominent socialites from the Washington community and a well-respected art critic from a national newspaper, all in the same room with my work, and all of it for nothing. The only thing anyone is going to remember is the murder of the gallery owner."

"Yes, there's that." It seemed odd that her first thought was for her own reputation as an artist rather than the death of someone she knew well. Although in a way I could relate to those feelings as I thought back to our first big gig for *A Fine Fix* last July and how a dead body had brought the evening to a screeching halt. I, too, had worried about the fate of our business.

Stopped at a red light, Rose rested her forehead against the steering wheel. Her voice came out in a strangled whisper. "Christine. Oh my god. Poor Christine." Her eyes were moist when she turned her head to me. "I don't know what I'm going to do without her."

I didn't know quite what to say. What did she mean by that? Was she referring to Christine's help in showcasing her art work? Or had there been something going on between the two of them? I'd seen them together last night, first arguing, then with heads together deep in conversation. Rose, in fact, had given Christine that magnificent pendant to wear at the opening. "She meant a lot to you," I ventured.

She nodded and, prompted by the honk of the car behind her, sat up straighter and accelerated through the intersection, saying nothing else.

Not ready to give up yet, I asked, "Who do you think would do something like that to her?"

Rose shook her head. "I don't know. Christine was one of the most prominent art dealers in town. A showing at her gallery could launch a career. I could name several local artists she helped to make it big." Stopped at another traffic light, Rose turned to me. "Of course she had enemies; other dealers, artists she had refused to promote. You saw that woman barge in last night. I'm sure she wasn't the first one shunned by Christine."

"The question is," I said, "Who would hate her enough to kill her?"

Rose turned away from me and repeated, "I don't know."

We pulled into the parking lot of a non-descript cement block building. A few others had already parked and were heading toward the entrance with their dogs.

Rose opened the back door and snapped a leash onto Zeus's harness, which he wore instead of a collar. He jumped down from the car and wagged his tail, looking eager to join his friends for agility training.

Inside, several people had set up camp, so to speak, in the spectator area that surrounded the arena, their coats, bags and other paraphernalia piled on seats. Several dogs yipped at each other, and one in particular, a small terrier of some kind, wouldn't stop barking, letting the others know not to mess with him.

I followed Rose and Zeus to an area where we shed our coats and bags and set up the three canvas chairs Rose had pulled from the trunk of the car. Zeus barked his arrival to the others, but a hand signal from Rose stopped him. He jumped up onto one of the chairs and sat obediently, but I could see by the spark in his eyes and his expectant panting that he was impatient to get out into the arena.

"Good boy," Rose said, pulling out a dog biscuit and giving it to Zeus.

Rose exchanged friendly waves and greetings with others. A young man in a plaid flannel shirt and jeans brightened when he saw her and headed our way. He looked to be in his mid-twenties, a nice-looking guy with a cleft in his square chin and blond hair that swept down over earnest hazel eyes. His unbuttoned shirt hung loosely over a t-shirt that revealed a lean but muscular physique. "Hey, Rose. Looking forward to watching Zeus compete on Sunday. He'll blow them all away."

She gave him a wide smile. "Hi, Sam. We're working on it. This is my friend, Trudie," she said, gesturing to me. "Sam helps train the dogs and preps them for competitions."

"Hi," I said.

"Hi." He barely acknowledged me before turning back to Rose, his shoulders hunched and thumbs linked into his jean pockets. "Listen, Rose, how about a cup of coffee after practice today?"

"Sorry." She shook her head. "Can't today. Working on a new sculpture."

The light in his eyes dulled. "Oh. Next time maybe."

"Maybe." She bent down to unzip her duffel bag, an obvious gesture of dismissal.

"Nice meeting you, Sam," I said as he turned to leave.

"Oh. Yeah," he said without even glancing my way and returned to the ring.

That feeling of being invisible to men still stung. After all these years, I should have been used to it by now. I'd learned that lesson well in high school and college. Stand next to a pretty girl and you are invisible.

"I guess this competition on Sunday is a big deal," I said.

"A very big deal," Rose said. "Zeus is one clean run away from earning a MACH title."

"What's that?" I asked.

"Master Agility Champion. Right now, he's at the Elite level, but on Sunday, Zeus will have earned enough championship points to achieve MACH status." She nuzzled into his coat and then kissed the top of his head. "Ready for your MACH run, huh Zeus?"

Zeus looked up at her then out toward the ring, panting with anticipation.

I could understand why he was so anxious to get out there. The arena, shaped like a huge oval the size of an ice rink, resembled a playground with assorted pieces of equipment, slides, tunnels, and hurdles, set out on a dirt floor.

Sam stood in the center of the arena instructing a woman on how to navigate her German shepherd through the course. Her dog was easily distracted and kept running back and forth across the ring. Next, a collie and his master took their turn, evidently a little more familiar with the circuit than the first participants. This time, Sam stood on the sideline and called out instructions. This dog did fairly well, ascending and descending the slide and scrambling through the tunnel but occasionally bypassing the hurdles.

"Next in line," Sam announced. "Zeus."

Rose led her dog into the arena and removed his harness. Murmurs of anticipation rustled through the spectator section as if they were awaiting the arrival of a flaming Baked Alaska. Then silence took over as Rose held out her hand for Zeus to stay in place. He didn't move. Sam took a seat on a bench to watch. Rose pointed to the first hurdle then ran alongside as Zeus easily flew over the obstacle. He turned the corner and sped through a long tunnel, then ducked under a hurdle. Turning the next corner, he climbed up an incline and slid down the other side, then wove in and out of a row of cones. Running beside him, Rose gestured to each piece of equipment and Zeus knew exactly what to do, performing his movements with perfection.

I found myself sitting on the edge of my seat, my heart pounding as the two of them maneuvered their way around the track, Zeus as professional as a circus dog and Rose graceful as a gazelle, both as skilled as chefs in a James Beard competition. I jumped up and down and hooted along with the other spectators. When they finished the course, everyone applauded and Rose knelt to caress her dog and give him a biscuit. Then she replaced his harness and led him out of the ring.

"Wow, that was incredible," I said as Rose and Zeus returned to their seats. I bent down and took the dog's face in both hands. "Zeus, you are a star."

He looked back at me, panting, his eyes bright with pride in his performance.

Rose retrieved a towel from her tote bag and wiped at the glistening perspiration on her neck and chest. Her tank top clung to her body, accentuating the curve of her breasts and protrusion of nipples. I turned to see if others noticed and, sure enough, both male and female dog owners and trainers were watching with rapt attention. When I glanced down at the ring, I wasn't surprised to see Sam, standing with hands in his pockets, his gaze focused on Rose.

As I shrugged into my coat, I looked at her again, wondering what it must feel like to have people constantly gawking at you. She seemed unaware of the attention, but more likely had learned to adopt an air of nonchalance. On the other hand, she had chosen to come braless and knew very well how she looked. So maybe she purposely sought out the attention.

"Thanks for inviting me," I said when Rose dropped me off at my car. "It was such a thrill to watch you both perform."

"I should thank you for the company. It's not too often Zeus gets to show off for people not associated with agility training."

Hearing his name, Zeus poked his head between the two of us, panting.

"Shake Trudie's hand," Rose said.

He picked up a paw and I shook it. "Nice to meet you, too, Zeus." Then I got in my car and headed to work.

My excitement had barely subsided as I pulled into a space at work next to Zach's car. I was anxious to tell him about my day.

"Hey, Zach," I called out as I entered.

"Hey." He stepped into the office from the warehouse. "Are you okay? When I left the gallery last night, you seemed really freaked out."

I shuddered, picturing Christine's dead body for the hundredth time. I'd enjoyed my morning off so much that I had pushed last night's events to the back of my mind. Now the memory stung my senses like the bitter scent of garlic sautéed too long in hot oil. "Who wouldn't be freaked out after what we witnessed?"

He nodded. "I know. I couldn't wait to pack everything up and get out of there last night.

I hope you didn't mind my leaving you there on your own."

"Not at all. You and Gordon did all the hard work. I didn't do a thing to help. I should be apologizing to you. Anyway, Daniel was with me, so I wasn't alone. And after a good night's sleep, I'm a lot better today."

"I'm glad. By the way, thanks for getting that design to us this morning. Good idea Rose had scanning it to us. You should see that wedding cake. It looks spectacular. I'm getting pretty good at working with fondant icing. Jennifer has taught me well." His eyes shone, reminding me of Zeus after he'd run the course.

"Can't wait to see it." I sat down at my desk, opened a drawer and pulled out the wedding file.

"How was your morning?" Zach sat in a chair facing me.

"Spent it at agility training."

"Huh? What's that?"

I smiled. "Kind of a dog version of *Iron Chef*." I filled him in about my excursion with Rose and Zeus.

"Sounds like something I'd like to see." He frowned. "How's Rose doing after last night?"

I sat back in my chair and sighed. "She's upset. I just can't figure out if she's more disturbed about Christine's murder or by the fact that her art showing was ruined."

"Were she and Christine close?" Zach asked.

"I can't figure that out either, and she was pretty close-mouthed about it."I frowned, thinking about the spiral pendant that had killed Christine and its duplicate in Jennifer and Rose's house.

"What's wrong?" Zach and I had been friends for so long we could often read each other's feelings.

I looked up at him. "Rose has a collection of metal-sculpted jewelry that she's made."

"And?"

"That spiral necklace Christine was wearing, the one that killed her..."

"Yeah."

"Rose made it for her."

Zach exhaled a big breath and dropped into the chair next to my desk. His eyes were wide. "Do you think she could have...?"

I shook my head. "I don't know, Zach. I just don't know."

Chapter Five

D aniel and I pulled up to Ally's new restaurant, *Savor*, and turned his car over to the complimentary curbside valet, a necessary service in a town like Bethesda, with over two hundred restaurants and parking at a premium.

While Daniel checked our coats, I surveyed the room with its cinnamon and navy décor, high ceilings and mixture of polished oak tables and warm upholstered booths. I recognized several of Ally's friends and her mom, Dana Schwartz, who sat in a booth opposite Barbara and Robert Lewis, the man who had funded this project.

"Hi, Mrs. Schwartz," I said, approaching her table. "Mr. and Mrs. Lewis."

"Trudie, dear. So nice to see you." Dana Schwartz put down her cocktail and held her arms out to me. I knelt to give her a hug, getting a whiff of bourbon, her preferred scent.

"You remember Daniel," I said, gesturing behind me.

"Yes, I do. Hello, Detective Goldman." Her smile faded, and I could tell she was remembering that fateful night we had both met Daniel for the first time when he'd come to investigate her husband's murder.

Daniel nodded. "Mrs. Schwartz. Good to see you."

"Trudie," Barbara Lewis said. "I'm thinking of having another dinner party. The last one you catered was wonderful. I'll call you soon."

"Sure," I said and handed her a business card from my pocket. "Zach and I would be happy to work with you again."

I heard someone call my name and spotted Ally approaching me, her arms wide for a hug. She glowed like a candle on a birthday cake, her long blonde hair bright against her fitted navy blue dress.

I hugged her, feeling the silkiness of her hair against my cheek. "Ally, this place is gorgeous." I stood back, my hands on her shoulders. "Your dad would have been so proud."

She nodded, her eyes moist. "I know. I wish he could have been here. This time I'm not going to trust this place to anyone else the way I did with the last one."

We looked at each other, remembering her father, who she'd been so close to before his untimely death last summer.

Zach came up behind her, put his arm around her shoulders and leaned down to give her a kiss. He had arrived early to help out with all the little details of a first night opening. I beamed at the two of them, so happy they had finally gotten together.

"So are we going to be seated or what?" I asked. "I can't wait to taste your food."

Ally had conceived *Savor* as the first in a chain of restaurants featuring a healthy comfort food menu. In a region like the Nation's

Capital, where most people wanted fresh, farm-to-table options but still loved their fried chicken and mashed potatoes, an establishment like this could easily be a great success.

As Ally led us to our table, I had a good feeling about this restaurant, the table layout, the warm lighting, the wonderful aromas and the cheerful buzz emanating from the diners. I turned to Ally. "I haven't even tasted your food yet, but I think you've got the magic ingredients here. I can feel it in my bones."

Ally stopped and took both my hands. "Do you really think so, Trudie? That means so much, coming from you."

I glanced around and nodded. "I really do."

Seated in a booth, Daniel and I ordered Caprese Bloody Marys, the tomato juice blended with spices and vodka, topped with a garnish of speared basil leaf, prosciutto and a mozzarella ball.

"How was your morning off?" Daniel asked, taking of sip of his cocktail.

"Interesting. I went to agility training with Rose and Zeus." I dug into the bowl of spiced nuts in the center of our table and munched on a few.

"You went where with who?"

I told him about my visit to Jennifer and Rose's house and the excursion to agility training and then about the metal jewelry and the duplicate spiral pendant.

Daniel frowned. "Trudie, I wish you hadn't gone over to that house."

"I had to. It was for business. I told you, Jennifer needed that sketch to decorate the wedding cake, and she couldn't get hold of Rose." I peered into my glass, retrieved the mozzarella ball, and popped it into my mouth, savoring its creamy goodness saturated with the spicy tomato and vodka mixture.

"But you didn't have to go with Rose to that agility thing. Trudie, I'd like you to stay away from that woman." He took a large gulp of his drink, the space between his eyebrows furrowed.

"Why? Is she a suspect?"

"Right now everyone is a suspect." He reached over and put his hand on mine. "I'd just feel a lot better if you kept away from the people who were there last night and let us do our job. I love you, Trudie, and I don't want you to get into a situation you can't get out of. Okay?"

My heart lurched every time he said those three words to me, something no man had ever told me before. "Okay."

He smiled, picked up his glass and kicked back the rest of his cocktail.

Our dinners came out next. Daniel had chosen the turkey breast, mashed acorn squash and roasted, caramelized Brussels sprouts. Anticipating Thanksgiving just the next week at my parents' house, I opted for oven-fried chicken with whipped cauliflower and sugar snap peas. We both finished off dinner with baked apples topped with a brandied whipped cream and toasted pecans. Everything was delicious. In no way did I feel as if I'd just eaten a health-conscious meal, but evidently I had.

At home in bed that night, I snuggled against Daniel. I loved the lingering musky scent of his aftershave and the firmness of his muscular chest and arms. In his protective embrace, I felt safe from sharp, deadly weapons, violent murders, and insolent interrogations. He pulled me on top of him and I straddled his waist, leaning forward to kiss him. He ran one hand down to the small of my back and the other through my hair, responding with his own urgent kiss.

An insistent buzz caught my attention, and I lifted my head to see my cell phone vibrating across the bedside table.

Daniel pulled me down to him and murmured, "Don't answer it."

The buzzing continued until I pushed myself off him. "I have to at least see who it is. It's late so it must be something important."

Daniel groaned.

I checked the screen on my phone which read "J. Hall." Jennifer? Why would she be calling now? She usually goes to sleep early to be at the coffee shop before sunup each morning.

"Trudie," she said, breathing hard. "I'm sorry to call so late but I need to get the number of that lawyer you know. What's his name?"

"Alan Bernstein. But why do you need a lawyer?"

"It's for Rose. She's been arrested."

I turned to Daniel and gave him a quizzical look. "Rose? Arrested? For what?"

"She's been arrested for Christine's murder. Now please, Trudie, give me that number for Mr. Bernstein."

"Sure. I'm getting it now." I retrieved my purse from the dresser and rummaged around in it until I found Alan's card. I read the number off to Jennifer. "Tell Alan you're a friend of mine and keep me posted, okay?"

"Okay. Thanks, Trudie."

Daniel sat up against the pillows, looking down at his hands.

"You knew about this, didn't you? Even when I was telling you at dinner about my visit with Rose, you knew she was going to be arrested. Didn't you?"

He lifted his head and sighed. "Yes, I knew."

I put my hands on my hips. "Then why didn't you tell me? I could have at least prepared the two of them for this. Jennifer is a friend and a business associate."

"That's exactly why I couldn't tell you, baby. You know I can't mix my professional with my personal life. Besides, any word to Rose could have caused her to run."

"But Rose? Why Rose?" I began to pace around the room. "What possible evidence could they have against her?"

Daniel put his legs over the side of the bed so his feet touched the floor. "Why not Rose? You told Will that you'd overheard her and Christine arguing."

"Will? Who's Will?" I didn't remember speaking to anyone named Will.

"Officer Billings. He has your interview on tape. You told him Rose was disputing something in her contract with Christine."

Oh, Bill Billings. That rude rookie cop who wouldn't take the time to listen to anything else I had to say. Will, not Bill.

I stopped pacing and put my hands on my hips. "Are you saying that I'm responsible for Rose's arrest?" My voice was shrill.

Daniel stood and came over to me, putting his hands on my shoulders. "No, of course you're not responsible for her arrest. There was other evidence, including her fingerprints all over the pendant."

I twisted away from him and took a step back. "Of course her prints were all over the pendant. She made that pendant for her. I even saw Rose adjusting it around Christine's neck."

"Trudie, calm down." Daniel took a step toward me and I backed up again.

"No. I don't want to calm down. There were other conversations I overheard that night, things that your friend, Bill—I mean Will Billings had no time for when he interviewed me. And here he's arresting Rose without even having all the evidence."

"Trudie, I don't understand why you're defending Rose like this," he said, holding his hands out to me. "You just met her for the first time last night. You don't know anything about her."

I turned away and folded my arms. Why was I defending her? Maybe I didn't want to be the one responsible for her arrest. Maybe I felt guilty because she was Jennifer's partner, and Jennifer was my friend and I trusted her choices. Or maybe, after spending the morning with Rose and seeing her relationship with Zeus, I was beginning to like her.

I turned around to face Daniel again. "Okay. What's done is done. But I'd like to be able to finish my interview with Officer Billings. I think he'll be very interested to hear what else I have to tell him. Can you arrange that for me?"

"Deal." He held his hand out to shake. When I took it, he pulled me close and bent his head for a kiss. "Will you come back to bed now?"

I wrapped my arms around his neck and kissed him back. "Deal."

Chapter Six

Wedding day. Well, not my wedding day, but a day I was determined to make special for the bride and groom. This would be the first large-scale wedding for *A Fine Fix*. It was important to get our name out and build a reputation in the bridal business world.

I arrived at work early that morning, and Zach was due in soon after a run to the Union Market in northeast DC for fresh fish, meat and produce. On the way back, he would pick up the wedding cake from Jennifer's coffee shop on U Street.

I made a quick call to the agency to confirm the number of bartenders, servers, and kitchen help we would need. With the ceremony beginning at six o'clock, followed by cocktails and dinner, I also made it clear that the hired staff must arrive at the mansion no later than three.

Zach and I spent the late morning and early afternoon prepping for the wedding, seasoning baby lamb chops, wrapping water chestnuts in brown sugar-coated bacon, and preparing mini crab cakes, all to be either grilled, roasted or broiled at the venue. The rockfish and filets would be seasoned right before cooking, and the baby vegetables and tri-color potatoes swabbed with olive oil, salt and pepper before roasting.

This had always been my favorite part of catering, working side-by-side with Zach. We'd been cooking together for so long—since childhood, in fact—that we'd developed a natural rhythm between us. It was easy and comfortable.

Zach looked over at me as he mixed the lump crab meat with our distinctive combination of spices that highlighted our crab cakes. "So have you heard anything about Rose? When will she be released?" he asked.

"I don't know. I've been waiting for a call from Jennifer. She was going to contact Alan Bernstein to represent Rose. But no word yet."

"If anyone can get Rose out of jail, it's Alan," Zach said. "I know that first hand."

"You're right," I said. "But I can barely stand the wait. I've got to find out what's going on."

With food preparations out of the way and everything packed into the cooler, Zach took the van to pick up the liquor order, and I tried to reach Jennifer again. The call went to voice mail, so I contacted Alan directly.

"Trudie, what a nice surprise." I could hear the smile in Alan's voice. "How long has it been?"

"A while," I said. "You know me. I only call when I need you." This was true. I had needed Alan's professional help twice last summer. He was a good lawyer, someone I could always count on. I liked Alan, but his interest in me went beyond friendship, something that didn't sit well with Daniel. So I'd kept my distance.

He chuckled. "You're calling about Rose Mendez, I assume."

"Yes. What's going on with her?"

"She should be released tomorrow afternoon."

"Tomorrow? She has to spend another night in jail? Why?"

"Just a couple of glitches to work out."

"What glitches? Usually, they can just post bail and will be released. What's the problem?" I seemed to be becoming familiar with the ins and outs of the court system.

He laughed again. "Trudie, I'm good but not that good. I know you're used to instant gratification when it comes to my services, but sometimes things take a little longer."

I felt the color rise to my face and was glad he wasn't here to witness it.

"But listen," Alan said. "Let's meet for coffee and catch up on our lives. Have some time today?"

I hesitated. Asking Alan to help Rose was one thing. Getting together with him on a personal level was another. I enjoyed Alan's company but didn't want to encourage his amorous interest. "Can't today. Zach and I are catering a wedding this evening. Too much to do."

"Maybe tomorrow or Monday then," he persisted. "I'd love to see you, Trudie—as a friend. Nothing more."

Alan understood my reluctance. But it would be nice to see him again. "Not sure about tomorrow. Maybe Monday. Give me a call."

"Perfect."

"And Alan, about Rose."

"No worries. I've got it under control. She'll be out by tomorrow afternoon."

No sooner had I hung up with Alan when Jennifer returned my call.

"How's Rose?" I asked.

"Rose is a strong woman. That's one of the things I love about her. She'll be fine, but I'm a basket case."

"I'm so sorry, Jennifer. I just spoke with Alan Bernstein, and he says she'll be out on bail tomorrow afternoon. He said there were some glitches about releasing her today. Do you know what they were?"

"It seems the judge on call is not keen on same-sex relationships, so he's dragging his feet. Mr. Bernstein said the judge who's on tomorrow is much more liberal and there shouldn't be a problem."

I felt the heat rise in my body like an oven thermometer. "But that's discrimination. In today's day and age—"

"In today's day and age," Jennifer said, "A lot of people still aren't comfortable with the LGBT issue. Rose and I encounter these things every day. That's the reality."

"Well, it's not fair." I hammered my fist on my desk so hard the folder of wedding paperwork bounced.

"Life isn't fair, but at least Rose and I can live together openly. In another place or time, we would have been stoned to death or burned at the stake."

"Okay, so she'll be released tomorrow afternoon. I guess that's not so bad in the scheme of things."

"Yes, tomorrow afternoon. But Rose is really upset. The timing couldn't be worse."

"Timing for what?" I asked.

"Zeus has an agility training competition tomorrow morning, and with Rose in jail, he won't be able to compete."

"Oh, yeah," I said. "That's a shame. He's so good out there in the ring. Isn't there someone else who can run the course with Zeus? Someone who works at the arena or another dog owner?"

"Trudie, this is a competition. The arena staff is only allowed to help during a practice session. And the other dog owners are Rose's competitors. He's supposed to achieve MACH status tomorrow. If Zeus doesn't run, he and Rose will have to wait until next year's state championship competition."

"Oh no. That's terrible." I stood up and began to pace back and forth.

"Rose has been wracking her brain to come up with someone to run the course with Zeus. She says anyone could do it; he knows it so well, he could run it himself, if that wasn't against the rules."

"What about you, Jennifer? Can't you do it?"

"If I could, I would. But I haven't watched them in the agility ring for quite some time. I barely remember anything about it. I also have a coffee shop to run. Sunday morning is our busiest time of the week."

Like steam being released from a pressure cooker, I blurted, "What about me?"

"What about you?" Jennifer asked.

"I could run the course with Zeus. I watched them yesterday. All Rose did was run the circuit with him and point to each piece of equipment. I could do that. I know I could."

"I don't know," Jennifer said. "You only watched them once. Rose has been training with Zeus for years."

"But Rose told you Zeus could run the circuit by himself. All he needs is a human to run along with him. I can do that." I swallowed hard. What was I doing? Where was this bravado coming from? I never work out, don't take walks. I wasn't even sure I would have the stamina to run around that entire arena or keep up with Zeus.

"Well," Jennifer said, sounding doubtful. "Let me ask Rose about this. If she thinks you can do it, then okay."

That afternoon, Zach and I headed to the wedding venue. The long driveway, flanked on both sides by stately pine trees, opened up to expose a huge southern-style mansion reminiscent of Tara in *Gone With The Wind* with its row of columns along the front porch.

Zach pulled the van around to the back kitchen entrance where we brought our supplies inside and unpacked them, first getting the perishables into the commercial-sized refrigerator, then placing the wedding cake in an isolated area where it wouldn't be disturbed. Next, we organized our work space for optimum efficiency.

A young woman holding a clipboard breezed into the kitchen. She had bouncy, shoulder-length chestnut hair, shiny and lush like the models you see on a hair color commercial. She stuck out her hand to me. "You must be Trudie Fine. I'm Cassie, the wedding planner. Please let me know if I can help with anything."

I shook her hand. "Well," I said, looking around me, "We might need help with the dirty dishes later."

She threw her head back and laughed, her fuchsia pink lipstick matching the blouse she wore beneath a light grey jacket and skirt. "You're funny, Trudie. But really, call if you need anything."

When the staff arrived from the agency, we were ready for them.

"Miss Fine?" I heard from behind me.

I turned, surprised to see Gordon, our server from the art gallery opening. I wondered whether he'd recovered from the events of the other night. "Gordon, how are you? And please, call me Trudie."

He stood awkwardly with his hands to his sides, clenching and unclenching his fists. "I'm okay, I guess."

He didn't look okay. His expression was troubled. I walked over to him and put my hand on his shoulder. "Are you sure?"

We looked at each other for a moment, perhaps sharing the horrific memory of Christine Dugan's dead body.

"Yeah. I think so," he said. "Sorry I made that big mess at the gallery. You know, with the wine and glass all over the place."

Again I felt like a mother with this young man who was still trying to spread his wings in the world. "Gordon, you don't have to apologize. Anyone would have done the same thing after witnessing what you had. Anyway, you're here now to help out, and I'm glad. So let's get to work."

I walked him into the ballroom. A couple of men who I assumed worked at the mansion were busy setting up round dining tables and chairs, while Zach was instructing the agency staff on how to arrange the place settings using a pre-set sample table. I was pleased to see the effect of the sheer white tablecloth over a gold liner that draped to the floor. Each place setting comprised a white bone china dinner plate rimmed with gold scrollwork and sitting atop a gold charger. The floral centerpiece had delicate gold branches that coiled up through an arrangement of white hydrangeas and lavender roses in a tall fluted glass vase.

A half hour later, when I stepped into the ballroom, our crew had covered all the tables with the linens and arranged the place settings. I watched Gordon as he artfully fanned cloth napkins and set them on plates. I might start requesting him for our jobs. He had the raw material to mold into something special.

The bridal party arrived with squeals and laughter, and bustled upstairs to get dressed. Their nervous excitement rang out from above and trickled down the circular stairway like glaze drizzled onto a Bundt cake.

Chairs were set on three sides of the huge foyer area for guests to view the ceremony, and lavender and white flowers cascaded down the banisters. Cassie stood at a polished credenza arranging the place cards in alphabetical order.

As I headed toward the sunroom, my cellphone rang.

"Trudie Fine?" the woman's voice asked.

"Yes."

"This is Amy Dugan. From the gallery."

"Oh, Amy. Hello." The last time I'd seen her, she had been sobbing into Rick's arms. "How are you?"

"All right, considering." She did, in fact, sound all right.

"What can I do for you?" I asked, stopping in the hallway to admire the wedding cake. The new woven pattern Jennifer and Zach had created on two of the layers looked amazing.

"In all the chaos of the other night, I realized we hadn't made your final payment. If you stop by the gallery, I can pay you the balance of what we owe."

"Well," I said. "I'd planned to send you an invoice after things…settled down. You can just put the check in the mail to me. Wouldn't that be easier for you?"

"Not really. I'm so overwhelmed by paperwork and making all the arrangements for poor Aunt Christine…" Her voice broke. "Do you think you can stop by to pick it up?"

I thought about Daniel's admonition to stay away from all the parties involved with the gallery opening.

"Well," I said again. "I'm catering a wedding all day today and have plans tomorrow. I've got a pretty busy week."

"Truthfully, Ms. Fine, I have something to tell you—about the other night."

"Something to tell me? I'm not the police. Why don't you tell them?"

"I'd like to speak with you directly. It's a…private matter."

I wondered what private matter Amy Dugan would have to speak to me about. I'd only spoken with her once on the phone and met her for the first time the night of the gallery opening. Maybe she would tell me something that would shed light about the killer. Then I'd be able to clear Rose. Daniel was not going to like this one bit, but how else was I going to get paid if Amy wasn't willing to put the check in the mail?

"Okay," I said. "Why don't I stop by early in the week, before Thanksgiving?"

"Sure. Just give me a heads up before you come."

As I pressed the *off* button on the phone and turned the ringer off, I thought it strange that Amy would go to the trouble of calling me to pay her balance. But it seemed she had more than just a payment on her mind. Why she wanted to reveal a private thought to me, I had no idea.

In the sunroom, which ran along the back of the mansion, tall windows with French doors spanned the width of the room and opened up to a spectacular view of a pristine lake, populated with white swans, rolling hills, and, like a backdrop in a landscape painting, Sugarloaf Mountain. Small cocktail tables and high tops scattered the room along with other random seating options. Zach was making sure the bars, located one at each end, were fully stocked, and the bartenders were busy slicing lemons and limes and lining up their mixers.

Zach turned to me, and we exchanged a smile. We'd come a long way, and it had taken a few years to get to this point. We knew that this event would be the one to propel our business into the future.

Cassie, the wedding planner, bounced into the room, a little breathless. "Everything looks lovely. You've done a marvelous job." She approached Zach and held out her hand to him. "I'm Cassie." She smiled, her pink lips looking newly refreshed. At events like this, women tended to be drawn to Zach, tall and striking in his black suit and purple silk tie.

He returned the smile and shook her hand. Having been an outsider in school like me, Zach was often surprised at this attention.

A buzz of arriving guests at the front entrance drew Cassie's attention. "Gotta run," she said and bounced out of the room.

My cellphone vibrated in my pocket. Who was calling me now? I wondered, pulling it out.

"Trudie, it's Jennifer."

"Jennifer, is everything okay?"

"Yes, nothing's changed. Rose should still be released tomorrow afternoon. I just wanted you to know that I went to see her and let her know you'd volunteered to do the agility competition with Zeus tomorrow."

Oh yeah. I'd forgotten all about that. "And what did Rose think?" I asked.

"She loved the idea, said you're a natural. She wants you to do it."

I swallowed, my original bravado sinking like a tea bag in boiling water. "She does, huh?"

Jennifer continued, talking fast. "Now I know you and Zach are at the wedding right now, so I'll email you all the instructions, directions to the arena, what to expect, and I'll leave all the equipment you'll need for Zeus in the mud room. You'll have to bring his crate this time. All the dogs are kept in a waiting area in their crates." She rattled out a few more instructions and then said, "Rose said just to do your best and Zeus should do just fine. Good luck, Trudie."

I stood a moment in stunned silence, as still as a flat soda. Well, I'd put myself into this situation so I would just have to go through with it. For now, I had a wedding to cater.

With the *hors d'oeurves* under control in the kitchen, I stepped into the hallway to watch the proceedings. The guests seated in the foyer buzzed with anticipation as a string quartet playing chamber music added an air of formality. I noticed a small flurry of activity at the top of the double curved stairway. Then the wedding party descended, bridesmaids in lavender cocktail dresses on one stairway, and groomsmen in gray tuxedos, on the other. As they took their places at the altar alongside the groom, the strings paused a moment then began the bridal march.

I looked up, and my breath hitched. The bride, in her magnificent white gown, paused at the top of the steps for everyone to see. Her blonde hair was coiffed in an upsweep, and she held a lovely bouquet of white hydrangeas and lavender roses.

As she proceeded down the stairs, in step with the music, tears sprang to my eyes. It wasn't just the beauty of the moment or the significance of the event. It was that, for the first time in my life, I could visualize myself as a bride. Of course, at only four months together, my relationship with Daniel was still fairly new. But this was the first time I'd had someone who actually loved and cared for me. Me, Trudie Fine. Fatty Fine. The joke of the senior class.

The bride's father, beaming with pride, met her at the bottom of the stairs and handed her over to her husband-to-be. I could see my own father and mother on my special day and the glint of a possibility that someday this could be me.

Chapter Seven

I woke early on Sunday morning, content with the success of the wedding. The bride and groom and their families had nothing but praise for our work, and several guests had requested business cards.

When I opened my eyes, Daniel lay propped on an elbow and was looking down at me. "Hi, beautiful." He brushed the hair out of my face with his fingers and bent to kiss my forehead.

"Hi, handsome," I said, smiling back at him. "Are you off today, too?"

"Sure am. Thought I'd take you out for brunch then down to the station this afternoon to speak to Will."

"Will who?" I asked.

"Officer Billings. Remember? You wanted to finish your interview with him."

"Oh, Bill Billings." Now it was Daniel's turn to look confused, and he cocked his head to one side. I giggled. "Never mind."

"Will said he can see you at about three. Okay with you?"

"Sure, that will work." Then I remembered my morning

commitment. "Oh, no," I said, hitting my forehead with the heel of my hand. "I can't do brunch. I told Jennifer I would stand in for Rose at the dog agility competition today. What was I thinking?"

"You're kidding? You, dog agility?" He laughed.

"Hey," I said, elbowing Daniel in the ribs. "What's so funny about that?"

"Well, I mean…you don't have a dog and you've only seen this agility stuff once. Couldn't Jennifer find someone else?"

"Apparently not. And it's all your fault anyway." I sat up and pushed Daniel down by the shoulders, my face a few inches from his.

"My fault? How?"

"You had Rose arrested. That's how. She won't be released on bail until this afternoon, and the competition starts at ten."

Daniel put his arms around me, rolled me onto my back and kissed me. "Then we've got a lot to do today, don't we? We'll just have to get started now."

I pulled him down for another kiss. "I guess so."

DANIEL AND I rounded Jennifer's house, and I found the hidden key in a planter on the back porch just where she had indicated. I unlocked the door and, remembering my previous surprise greeting from Zeus, I took hesitant steps through the mud room into the kitchen.

"Well hi, Zeus," I said as he approached me, his tail wagging.

When Zeus saw Daniel, he emitted a low growl, but Daniel stooped down and spoke in soothing tones. The dog approached him warily, and Daniel held out both hands for Zeus to sniff.

"Zeus, this is Daniel."

"Hi, Zeus. I've heard a lot about you." Daniel ran his hands over the dog's smooth coat, and Zeus licked his face.

"Okay," I said. "Now that we're all friends, let's go do this thing."

I knelt down and scratched Zeus behind the ears. Then I looked into his eager eyes. "We've got an important day ahead of us, boy. And I'm going to need your help. Okay?"

He panted then followed me to the container of dog biscuits. I put several into a Ziploc bag and gave one to Zeus.

Back in the mud room, Jennifer had left Zeus's crate which she'd instructed me to bring to the competition, but I wasn't sure why since he'd sat obediently in a chair with Rose and me at the agility training session. I retrieved the harness from a hook, and Zeus stood still as I struggled to put it on him. Then I attached the leash, grabbed the sports bag and, with Daniel carrying the crate, led Zeus out the back door and around to the front to Daniel's car.

A large banner above the entrance to the arena announced, "AKC State Agility Championship." The lot was so full we had to park several rows away from the entrance.

Inside the lobby area, I spotted Zach and Ally. "What are you guys doing here?"

"We thought you could use a cheering section," Zach said.

"You know I used to be a cheerleader in high school, so I brought all the accoutrements." Ally unzipped a pink duffel bag and extracted two blue and white pom poms and a sign that said, "Go Zeus."

"Wow," I said. "Thanks for coming."

Zeus sniffed inside the bag and when he lifted his head, had a nose covered with glitter. He shook his head and sneezed a few times.

"Oops," said Ally. "Didn't know that was in there." She stuffed everything back in the bag and zippered it up.

When we stepped into the arena, I held my breath. The viewing area was buzzing with activity. Most of the seats were occupied with people standing and talking with other participants or shouting to their children who were running up and down the aisles. Agility training had been nothing like this. I froze like a popsicle, wondering why in the world I had volunteered to do this. In front of all these people who'd been working with their dogs—the best in the state—for years.

A uniformed woman directed us down a hallway to the dog holding area. As we got closer, the barking became louder and louder. The room was filled with crates, about a hundred fifty of them, each containing a dog. I wondered how long the competition would take for all these dogs to run. A posting at the entrance to the room gave the lineup, which I soon realized was in alphabetical order. I ran my finger down the page to the very last listing, Zeus.

I noticed that some people stood next to their dogs' crates, evidently getting ready to take their places in line for their runs. Daniel and I found a spot for our crate in between two others and I knelt next to Zeus, who seemed unperturbed by the situation. "I guess you've done this before, boy," I said to him. "So you know the drill. We're going to have to leave you for a while. But at least you've got some friends to talk to." I indicated the crate to the left, which housed a collie, and to the one on the right with some sort of terrier. Zeus approached the crate where he and the terrier sniffed at each other. When I unlatched the door to his crate, Zeus calmly trotted inside and laid down on the neatly stacked padding and blankets cushioning the bottom.

"Good boy." I unhooked his leash and handed him a biscuit from my pocket. "I'll be back when it's time to line up."

Daniel took my hand and led me back into the arena where Zach and Ally waited. Then the four of us descended the stairs and settled into an empty row of seats. As I pulled off my jacket, Sam approached from a lower row, taking the stairs two at a time and tilting his head from one side to the other, his eyes searching behind me.

"Where's Rose?" he asked, barely bothering to glance my way.

"She's not here today," I said.

"Not here?" He looked up, his face stricken. "But this is the state competition. Zeus needs to compete. Where is she?"

"Not here," I repeated.

"But who...?

"I'll run the course with Zeus."

"You?" He looked at me good and hard, from top to bottom. "But you can't do that. You're..."

"She's what?" Daniel said, stepping between us.

Sam's face paled. "She's never done this before, and she's not signed in to run with Zeus."

Daniel put his hand on Sam's shoulder and squeezed. "Then you'll write her name in, won't you, bud? Trudie, give this young man a business card with your name."

I dipped my hand into my coat pocket, extracted a card and handed it to Sam. "Trudie Fine," I said smiling. "*A Fine Fix.*"

Sam nodded and headed toward the judges in the front row to make the change.

"Thanks." I reached up to give Daniel a peck on the cheek.

"For what?"

"For standing up for your woman and putting that jerk in his place."

"Are you?" Daniel's eyes twinkled.

"Am I what?"

"My woman."

"Yours and nobody else's," I said.

An announcement on the microphone that the proceedings were about to begin settled everyone down. We sat in our seats. "First up," the announcer said, "Ace." This was going to be a long competition.

One by one, dogs took their turns with near perfection. The handlers, too, each seemed to have a special bond with their dog, using their own unique hand signals when running the course. We sat through runs by Bailey, Boomer, Comet, a few Dukes, Finn, Jackson, Max, Parker, so many names, I lost track of them.

As I watched, my stomach churned so much, it could have made butter. How was I ever going to pull this off? Daniel, sitting next to me, tried to hold my hand, but I pulled it away and rubbed my palm back and forth on my jeans to dry it before reaching for his hand again. Next to him, Zach and Ally sat forward in their seats hooting with the rest of the audience at the performances. I leaned across Daniel toward Ally. "Hey, save all that energy for me and Zeus."

When they got to the S names, I could bear the wait no longer. "I can't sit still anymore," I said to Daniel. "I'm going to wait with Zeus. They'll want him to line up soon anyway."

Zeus stood when he saw me, sparking a few barks from neighboring crates.

An official approached. "You might want to take him outside for a moment."

"Huh?" I asked.

The young man rolled his eyes. "To relieve himself before his turn."

"Oh, yeah." I chuckled. "Wouldn't that be embarrassing in the middle of his run?"

I opened the crate and hooked his leash to the harness then escorted Zeus out the side exit door. I'd left my coat on my seat so the cold air sent a jolt through my system as if I was entering the walk-in cooler in our warehouse. It was a familiar sensation that calmed me as we walked along the grassy patch of ground lined with bushes.

When we returned to the holding room, I checked with the attendant who consulted the list and agreed that since we were up to Vader and then Winston, Zeus and I might as well stand near the end of the line.

As we waited, I looked at Zeus, who sat in rapt attention watching the proceedings. He reacted to my glance by dancing on his front paws, obviously ready to rumble and not a bit nervous. I leaned toward him and ran my hand over his coat. "Not our turn yet," I whispered.

Sooner than I'd hoped, the announcer called, "Final competitor, Zeus."

Oh my god, oh my god, oh my god kept going through my head as I led Zeus by the leash, or rather he led me, into the ring. *Okay focus*, I told myself. Just like in a catering job, this wasn't about me. It was always about and for the client, and Zach and I aimed to perform to their highest expectation. Today, I was representing Rose and would do my best for her and for Zeus. Never mind that, unlike catering, I was totally unqualified for this.

Zeus and I walked to the starting point, and I stopped and pointed at him the way I'd remembered Rose doing it. He sat.

"Good boy," I said, wanting to give him a biscuit but realizing I'd left them in the duffel bag at the seats. I stroked his head and murmured, "I promise you a biscuit when we're all done. Okay?"

His eyes shone and with his tongue hanging out, he looked like he was smiling. I took that as a good sign. I knelt to unfasten his halter and fumbled with the straps, feeling as if I were trying to roll sushi with ski gloves.

"Take your places, please," the announcer said.

I took a long breath and sent a prayer to the kitchen gods. Then the buzzer sounded and I began to run, pointing to the first hurdle. Zeus sailed over effortlessly. I pointed to the ramp, and up he climbed and pranced across the bridge, sliding down the other side. Then he rounded the barrel, ducked under a hurdle, and scampered through the tunnel.

In the background, I heard Ally yelling, "Z-E-U-S, Z-E-U-S, gooooooo Zeus!" There was no way I could look up into the audience, but I imagined her jumping up and down with her pom poms.

We weren't even halfway through the course and already I was winded. I'd worn tennis shoes, but I was unaccustomed to the feel of the dirt floor as I kicked up dust behind me.

Zeus was getting ahead of me now, jumping over three hurdles in a row. He glanced back at me as if to say, "C'mon. Can't you keep up?"

Still, I pointed to each obstacle as he approached them. When he wove in and out through a row of poles, it slowed him slightly so that I was able to catch up. Then he flew over a hurdle, scaled another ramp and slide, and maneuvered through a curved tunnel, darting out and under the final obstacle.

I heard an explosion of cheering and applause from the audience as I bent forward, supporting myself with my hands on my knees, and trying to catch my breath. Zeus danced around me in excitement. The female judge ran up to us, gave me a big hug, and handed me a huge yellow rosette with satin streamers and a hurdle bar decorated with long, colorful tassels on the ends. "Go ahead. Do your MACH run," she said with a twirl of her finger through the air.

MACH run? I thought. Didn't we just do that? I stood still, and the judge, realizing I was new at this, smiled and said, "A victory lap with Zeus around the ring."

Another run? I could barely breathe as it was. But I looked at Zeus and said, "Let's do it."

And we ran.

Zeus flew over a hurdle higher than I'd ever seen him do it before. Then he scampered through a tunnel and wove through the poles.

The audience whistled and hooted and clapped until we completed our run. I gestured for Zeus to sit then used my last ounce of energy to retrieve his halter. "Good boy," I said as he sat still while I adjusted it on his body and attached the leash. "Now let's get you a treat."

In the holding area, I reached into the duffel bag and pulled out a dog biscuit for Zeus. He sat obediently, but his body vibrated with excitement.

"We did good today, didn't we Zeus?" I said as I gave him his biscuit. His expression as he looked at me told me he knew exactly what I was saying.

I pulled a towel out of the bag to dry my face, neck and arms. I'd worn a cotton t-shirt, and now understood why Rose chose to dress so scantily for practice the other day.

"You both were great," Daniel said as he hugged me in the lobby. "I'm sorry I ever doubted you."

"Great?" Ally said. "They were awesome."

"Did they put up the run times yet?" I asked.

"Yes," Daniel said. "Not only did he earn his MACH title, Zeus came in third."

I looked down at Zeus, "Third place. We did it, boy, didn't we? Rose is going to be so proud of us."

"And I've got it all on tape for her to see," Zach said.

Daniel, Zach and Ally took Zeus and the crate outside while I packed our gear into the duffel bag. I heard someone behind me clear his throat and I turned.

Sam stood looking down at his feet. He sighed, raised his head and held his hand out to me. "Congratulations."

I held back a moment, remembering my other encounters with Sam and wondering if I should give him a taste of his own rotten fish. I decided to take the high road and extended my hand to his. "Thanks," I said.

"Um...sorry I was such an asshole before. It's just...just that you've never run the course before. And I was disappointed that Rose wasn't here. Is she okay?"

No way was I going to tell Sam that Rose was in jail on a murder charge. If she wanted him to know, that was her choice to tell him, not mine. "She's fine. Just a little under the weather. It probably wasn't the smartest idea for me to volunteer to run the course with Zeus, was it?" I huffed out a laugh.

He shook his head and grinned, his gaze for the first time focusing so directly into mine that, as much as I tried to resist, my heart skipped a beat. "No, probably not. But it worked. And on behalf of Rose, thank you."

Chapter Eight

Daniel and I met Zach and Ally at the sidewalk seating area of her restaurant for a celebratory lunch. The air was crisp but unseasonably warm for late November. Ally brought out a crustless quiche for us to share along with a buttery Chardonnay. Zeus lapped from a large bowl of water and hungrily downed a bowl of ground turkey and brown rice that the chef had cooked up for him.

"To Zeus," Zach said, holding up his wine glass in a toast. At the sound of his name, Zeus peered up, water dripping from the side of his mouth.

"To Zeus," we all chimed in, clinking our glasses together.

"And to Trudie." Daniel leaned over for a kiss, the amber in his eyes glinting. I lingered for a moment on his lips, their familiar taste mingling with the wine, and he put his hand behind my head to pull me closer.

My heart leaped like pine nuts toasting in a hot pan, by far outshining my blip of a reaction to Sam barely an hour before.

"Okay, you two," Ally laughed. "This is a family restaurant. Save it for later."

And "save it for later" we did. Once we had dropped Zeus off and were back at home, Daniel joined me in the shower. Only the knowledge that I had a three o'clock appointment with Officer Will Billings inspired us to dry off and get dressed.

At the station, Daniel left me, as he said, in Will's capable hands while he took the time to catch up on some paperwork. Billings' cubical was typical of this station, institutional green walls, a desk made from a cheap wood veneer, and two mismatched chairs. A four-drawer metal file cabinet stood in the corner and a couple of shelves bracketed to the wall held a collection of what looked to be police procedural books.

Unlike the other officers' work spaces, however, Will's folders were stacked neatly alongside the telephone. A generic white ceramic mug held half a dozen matching pens and three newly sharpened pencils. In the center of the desk, a yellow legal pad and pen sat atop a pristine calendar blotter that looked as if it had just been turned to the November page, not an entry in sight.

I thought of the calendar pad that sat on my desk at *A Fine Fix*. Already in the third week of the month, the page was covered with notes and doodles, the edges curled and the entire sheet stained and warped after multiple coffee spills.

"Hello, Trudie," Billings said with a quick nod.

No Miss Fine today? I wondered why he felt he could speak so informally with me. Billings, in fact, was dressed much more casually than before in a gray V-neck sweater layered over a light blue button-down shirt. That, along with his beige khakis and loafers, gave him a preppy appearance. Still, the pants were pressed with a sharp crease and the burgundy shoes polished to a high shine.

"No uniform today?" I asked.

"Day off." He pointed to a chair with a cracked black Naugahyde seat. Then he walked behind his desk and took a seat facing me.

"So you came in just to meet with me?" I asked.

Billings' posture was rigid, his chiseled features serious, unsmiling, his dark eyes focused only on me. He nodded. "Daniel asked me."

That was it. Daniel had asked him. No further explanation needed.

"Shall we get down to it, Trudie? I understand you have additional information that you think may shed light on the investigation, information you didn't share with me at our previous meeting. Is that right?"

"Correction. I have information you didn't give me a chance to share with you at our previous meeting. As I remember, you cut that meeting short."

His facial expression remained frozen, reminding me of an ice sculpture of an Indian chief, the centerpiece for an event we'd catered at the American Indian Museum downtown. "I believe I gave you ample time to answer my questions, Miss Fine."

Miss Fine. There it was. I felt the heat rise to my face. At the same time, I moved forward to the edge of my seat, leaned toward him, and spouted out my next sentence without taking a breath. "Officer Billings, if I remember correctly, in the middle of your questioning, you received a phone call and abruptly ended our meeting."

For a moment, he was silent. His jaw clenched, and a vein in his temple bulged. I almost felt as if I could read his mind as it wondered what in the world Detective Daniel Goldman saw in me. He released his breath with a whoosh, stood up and began to pace. After a moment, he came to an abrupt stop behind his chair and glanced down at me.

"I'm sorry, Miss Fine. I think we should begin again on a better note."

"Trudie," I said.

"Trudie." He sat down in his chair and nodded to me.

I relaxed a little and leaned back in my chair. "I overheard a conversation that night as I passed Christine Dugan's office. I think it might be significant."

Billings picked up his pen and nodded. "What did you hear, Miss—Trudie?"

"Christine was instructing her employees, Amy and Rick, to make two sales each that evening."

"And if they didn't make these sales?" Billings asked, jotting notes on the legal pad.

"She would fire them."

Billings raised an eyebrow. "And their response to Ms. Dugan?"

"Christine's niece, Amy, complained that no one would buy these 'monstrosities' as she called them. But Christine didn't care. She was adamant that they make the sales. She basically said the gallery wasn't doing well and she couldn't afford to keep the two of them on unless they brought in some income."

"And Rick? What was his reaction to Ms. Dugan?"

"I didn't hear him say anything to Christine in her office, but once he and Amy were out in the hall, he said something like, 'One person has to go, all right. And it isn't you or me.'"

"Do you think he meant that in a menacing way?"

"I don't know if he was being sarcastic or if he really meant it. Your guess is as good as mine."

Billings stared at me but seemed to be focusing somewhere else, processing the new information I'd just provided. Then he spoke. "I'm sorry, Trudie."

"For what?"

"For not affording you the opportunity to share everything with me the other night. You're right. I did cut our meeting short."

"But why?"

"The phone call I received confirmed my suspicions. I had a suspect and a motive, and now I had the physical evidence. I had my killer." He shook his head. "Daniel wasn't quite as convinced as I."

"Daniel was against the arrest?"

"He would have waited, taken more time for the investigation."

So Daniel didn't want to arrest Rose after all. And I had been so furious with him. I'd thought it was all his idea. All along it was this new guy, Billings, who'd pulled the strings. "You know, Officer Billings, you could learn a lot from a veteran detective like Daniel."

Billings colored. "You're right. He's good."

"So if Rose's arrest was a mistake, does that mean she isn't a suspect anymore?" I asked.

"No. It means everyone is a suspect, including Rose, until the investigation is over and the real murderer is brought to justice. Again, I'm sorry, Trudie, for not hearing you out the other day. Things might have gone differently if I had."

I guess this was my day to accept apologies.

When we were leaving the station, Daniel shook Billings' hand. "Thanks for taking time out of your day off. I'm sure you had better things to do today."

"Not really. No family in town. Just another quiet Sunday."

"Going home for Thanksgiving?" Daniel asked.

Billings reddened a little. "No. My parents are divorced, living in separate states. I don't see either of them very often."

"Then what are you doing on Thanksgiving?" Daniel persisted.

"I volunteered to come into work. Let the people with families enjoy their holidays."

Daniel glanced at me, and nudged me with his elbow. I knew what he wanted me to do.

"Bill—I mean, Will," I said. "Come have Thanksgiving dinner with us, at my parents' house."

"Oh, no. I can't impose. I don't even know your parents."

"Believe me, Will," Daniel said. "Nothing would make Trudie's mother happier than having more guests for Thanksgiving. There will be so much food she could probably feed this entire station. You've got to come."

"Well, to be honest, with so many of the guys looking forward to getting paid time and a half that day, they really didn't need me. And I don't remember the last time I had a homemade Thanksgiving dinner.

I'd like that." His grin was uncertain but the first smile I'd seen on his face.

"Great," Daniel said. "Come early. We'll watch some football, have a few beers." He slapped Will on the back and we left the station.

Walking to the car, I slipped my hand into Daniel's. He squeezed my hand and leaned over to plant a kiss on my forehead. My heart surged as I wondered what I did to deserve such a great guy.

Chapter Nine

I was boxing up leftovers from dinner while Daniel loaded the dishwasher when my phone rang.

"Trudie, it's Rose."

"Rose," I said, glancing at Daniel. "Are you home now?"

"Yes. Out on bail and home. I wanted to thank you for what you did for me—and for Zeus—today. I heard you were amazing out there in the ring."

I smiled. "Well, Zeus was amazing. I was just standing in as a poor imitation of you. I guess it was a bit of a stupid risk."

"No, not at all. If it weren't for you, Zeus would have had to wait until next year's state finals. You gave him a chance, and it paid off. You were extremely brave to do what you did. There was nothing stupid about it."

"I'm glad it worked out. It actually was a lot of fun working with Zeus."

"Trudie, I want to thank you properly. I have something for you. Can you stop by the house tomorrow?"

"Stop by?" I asked. "I don't know. I have to get into the office early tomorrow. We have a couple of jobs coming up this week."

Daniel slipped a dinner plate into a slot on the bottom rack then turned to watch me.

"Please, Trudie. I want to give you a token of my thanks. And Zeus would love to see you, too. I'd bring it to you, but I want you to choose the one you like best."

I stood with the phone to my ear looking at Daniel, a question on my face, knowing he wanted me to stay away from Rose. But why would she want to harm me? I was not a threat to her. In fact, her partner Jennifer provided baking services for our catering events. Not to mention, I had just done her a huge favor.

"I guess I can stop by this afternoon on the way to see a client. Will that work for you?" I asked, my eyes fixed on Daniel's.

"Great," she said. "See you then."

I pressed the *off* button.

"Not a good idea," Daniel said.

I walked over to him and put my hand on his arm. "She wants to give me something as a thank you. That's all. You know as well as I do that Rose is not a threat to me. I'll stop by for a moment and then leave. Okay?"

"I know no such thing. Rose is still a suspect. You need to stay away from her until this investigation is over." He put his hands on my shoulders. "Trudie, I can't let you see her."

I wrenched myself away from him. "Can't let me? You're my boyfriend, Daniel. Not my father. What? Are you going to give me a time out?"

"I just don't want anything to happen to you. It could be dangerous." He came toward me and held out both hands. "I don't want to lose you, Trudie. I love you."

There were those three words again. Words no man, except my father—and maybe my best friend Zach—had ever uttered. My heart soared.

"And I love you, Daniel. But you need to trust me and my instincts. Rose has no reason to hurt me. I'm going over there tomorrow afternoon."

Daniel exhaled a sigh of resignation and turned back to the dishwasher to load glasses in the top rack. "You're a grown woman, Trudie. You can make your own choices. Just be careful."

IN THE MORNING, at the office, Zach and I finalized the paperwork on Saturday's wedding and congratulated ourselves on a great event.

"I'd like to request Gordon again from the agency," I said. "He's a good kid and he really wants to learn."

"I agree." Zach was working on the computer entering the final numbers on a spreadsheet. "Did you see the care he took setting the tables and folding the napkins? But Trudie, are you sure you're not just feeling sorry for what he had to go through the other night?"

I sunk into the chair on the opposite side of the desk. "That's part of it, I guess. I do feel sorry for him. No one should have to go through what he did—discovering the victim of a gruesome murder. But also, at some point we may need to bring in a young trainee as our company grows."

Zach laughed. "Whoa, Nellie. Right now we're doing well. Very well, as a matter of fact. Bringing in a trainee is something that's a ways into the future. We've got lots of time for expansion. For now, we can handle things fine by ourselves."

"Just saying. In the meantime, we'll keep our eye on Gordon. By the way, Amy Dugan wants me to come by the gallery this afternoon to pick up our final payment."

"Why doesn't she put it in the mail?"

"I asked her the same thing. She insisted she wants to hand it to me in person."

"Won't it be weird going back to the scene of the crime?" Zach said. "Are you sure you want to go back there? I can pick up the check if you want."

"I suppose it will be a little creepy. But I might as well do it. I'm stopping to see Rose first. She wants to give me something to thank me for taking her place at the agility competition. After that, I'll head to the gallery."

FOR THE FIRST time, I entered Rose and Jennifer's house through the front door. The foyer was painted gray with white trim, and more of Rose's artwork adorned the walls, contemporary pieces similar to those exhibited at the gallery but softer scrolls of black on white and warm splashes of color like lemon and tangerine that felt welcoming.

Amy and Rick might have been more successful getting sales at the opening with works like these.

Zeus bounded up to me and danced with anticipation until Rose nodded that he could greet me. I held out my arms and knelt to meet his anxious and very wet greeting. I sunk my fingers into Zeus's smooth coat and peered into his moist eyes as we shared the memory of our victorious day. "Hey, fella," I said. "We had a spectacular day yesterday, didn't we?"

He gave his tail a fierce wag that caused his entire hind quarters to move back and forth.

"Okay, guys. Enough with the love fest." Rose signaled Zeus to sit, and he complied immediately.

"How are you holding up?" I asked Rose. "It couldn't have been easy being held in jail for the past few days.

Rose appeared more fragile than I'd seen her before. The robust artist and sculptor, the graceful gazelle in the agility ring, were gone. Her face was pale, and the gray hoodie and sweat pants she wore seemed to diminish her.

She lifted her chin. "I'm okay. They kept me warm and fed, gave me a bed to sleep on, caged me up with other women. Kind of like animals at the zoo."

I wrapped my arms around her shoulders and pulled her in for a hug. Her chin, buried in my shoulder, began to tremble, and I could feel the wetness of her tears saturate my blouse.

"Not that great, was it?" I asked.

She stepped back, holding onto my shoulders, and shook her

head. "No. It was demeaning and dehumanizing. I've spent my life building a career and a reputation and directing my life the way I wanted it to go. And it's all wiped out in an instant."

I took her hands in mine. "Wiped out in an instant, but only for an instant. You're home now, and you're still that same talented artist, the same strong woman you've always been, with people who care about you."

"Yeah. That's exactly what Jennifer said." She laughed. "But here I am sniveling all over you when I invited you here to thank you. Zeus earned MACH status and even came in third in the agility competition. That was amazing, what you did."

"Really, Rose. I was happy to do it. Scared to death, but how could I fail with a talented dog like Zeus? Now I can check it off my bucket list—agility training competition, check."Rose laughed. "I know that was never on your bucket list. Come with me," she said, leading me into the living room and stopping in front of the display of metal jewelry. "I want you to choose any piece you like."

Any piece I like? Just the thought of that spiral pendant caused me to catch my breath. At least, I noticed, the duplicate pendant I'd seen last time I was here, the one that matched the murder weapon, was missing. I shuddered.

"What's the matter?" Rose asked.

"It's just that…that—"

"You're thinking of Christine. Right?"

"Yes. I'm so sorry. Your jewelry is spectacular. And under other circumstances, I would be thrilled to wear one of your pieces. But it just brings me back to the other night…seeing her in her chair…the pendant." I couldn't finish. I didn't need to finish. Rose knew exactly what I meant.

She touched my arm. "God, Trudie. I invited you over to thank you, but all I did was upset you. I'm sorry."

She took my hand and led me through the living room and into an art studio, bright and sunny. An easel sat near the window, a table of palettes and brushes and paints close by. Several canvases of varying sizes, some framed, some not, leaned against the wall.

"I know just the thing for you." Rose walked along the wall, pulling the paintings forward until she spotted the one she wanted. "Yes, this is the one I'd like to give you." She picked up the small framed painting and turned it toward me.

Goosebumps broke out on my arms, and I felt a pang in my heart as I recognized a portrait of Zeus, his eyes bright and his tongue hanging to the side as if he was smiling for the artist. "You want to give this to me? Did you paint this? I mean, it's not anything like your other work."

"Yes, it's mine. Every once in a while, for something or someone important, I'll delve into realism. In fact, I'm working on a portrait of Jennifer." She beckoned me with her arm. "Come see."

Rose had captured Jennifer perfectly on the canvas with her chef's coat and the pink paisley bandana tied around her pixie hairdo.

"It's lovely," I said. I could see the love infused into this painting. I could also see the intensity in Jennifer's eyes as she looked at the artist.

I'd been holding the portrait of Zeus close to my chest, but now I held it out to her. "Rose, I'm sure you'll want to keep this painting of Zeus for yourself. I mean, I love it, but Zeus is your dog. This should be your memento."

"No, Trudie, I want you to have it. I can see the affection you have for Zeus. The two of you have a bond now."

I knelt down to Zeus who sat patiently by my side.

"What do you think, Zeus?" I asked, holding the painting out for him to see.

Shall I take this one?"

He licked my ear, and I considered it a done deal.

Chapter Ten

I pulled up the steep driveway at the Christine Dugan Gallery then backed into the alley where we'd parked our catering van the other night. Parking was non-existent in Dupont Circle, and my only other option was to drive around the block, checking side streets for residential curbside parking. My car was blocking two others, but I only planned to drop in for a minute to pick up the check.

The Gallery was closed on Mondays, and I thought I'd have to make my way down the incline around to the front door and ring the bell to get in. But surprisingly, the back door was propped open with a brick. Not wanting to walk in unannounced, I knocked on the door. "Hello," I called out. "Hello."

No one replied or came to the door, so I took tentative steps inside. "Hello? Is anyone here?" Of course, I knew someone was here because of the cars in the alley and the propped-open door. But it just seemed like the right thing to do.

The back door entered into the kitchen, so I had my bearings right away. I decided to proceed down the hall to Amy's office, the room where Officer Billings had first questioned me. After all, she was the one who had invited me to come. Her office, however, was devoid of everything except the furniture, the desk and shelves completely cleared. Not only was Amy not there. It seemed as if she had moved out.

A minute later, I heard footsteps heading my way down the hall. Rick rounded the corner holding a large carton. "Trudie," he said when he saw me. "What a nice surprise. Uh, excuse me."

I moved out of the way when I realized his intention was to carry the box into the empty office.

The sleeves of Rick's pullover fisherman's sweater were pushed up almost to his elbows and revealed tanned, muscular arms. He wore dark-washed jeans and boat shoes with no socks. He put the carton on the desk and turned to me with a big grin that showed his perfect white teeth. "To what do I owe the pleasure of this visit?" he asked.

For a moment, I felt engulfed by his gaze and by the clean, citrusy scent of his cologne. "Uh, I—actually, Amy asked me to come so she could give me a check for the other night."

"Well, Amy's here. Moved her things down the hall to Christine's and I'm evacuating the closet I'd been using as an office to get a little breathing space. Hope you don't mind," he said, pulling off his sweater. "I didn't realize how hot I'd get moving my belongings." A white t-shirt clung to his body displaying every ripple of muscle.

"It is a little warm in here." I felt my face flush and turned away from him. "So Amy is moving into Christine's office? Isn't it a little soon? I mean, Christine was Amy's aunt. When is the funeral?"

Rick's face became serious, and he stood more erect, towering over me. He was a few inches taller than Daniel, maybe six-foot-two, and I craned my neck to peer up at him. "The funeral is scheduled for Friday, the day after Thanksgiving. Black Friday. Funny, just thought of that. Weird, huh?"

Weird, maybe, I thought. But funny? "How's Amy doing?"

"Amy's a doer. She addresses every situation head on. So funeral scheduled. Check. Offices moved. Check. Business as usual. Check. I guess everyone has their own way of coping with tragedy. This is Amy's way." He walked behind the desk and began opening drawers, peering into each one, I supposed to see if they were empty or to assess how his belongings would fit.

Apparently forgotten now, I muttered, "Well, I'll get out of your way and go find Amy."

My progress down the hallway slowed the nearer I got to Christine's office. Every fiber of my body vibrated with apprehension, and I took it as a sign to turn around and leave the building and never look back. Sooner than I'd hoped, however, I found myself standing at the doorway and peered inside. It surprised me that, just like Amy's office, the shelves and desk top were completely cleared. Beams of sunlight streaked into the room highlighting a myriad of floating dust particles.

Much of the furniture was covered in a gray dust, which I realized was fingerprint powder left by the investigators. A few yellow balls of trash, I recognized as crime scene tape, clustered in the back corner of the floor.

I inched my way into the room, trying to shut out the vision of

Christine's impaled body reclining in her chair.

"Amy?" I whispered, afraid of whipping up a flurry of ghosts.

No answer.

Snap out of it, I told myself. You're just here to pick up a check and leave. There's no body, no blood. Only the residue of a crime scene.

I shuffled further into the room knowing Amy was not there. I stood stiffly, my back to the door, as if expecting her to materialize in front of me out of nothing.

"Trudie. There you are."

I jumped with a yelp.

She laughed. "Sorry. Didn't mean to startle you."

The awkward Amy I remembered from the other night with the boxy dress and clunky shoes looked different today, wearing tight jeans and a fitted pink sweater, her hair pulled back into a sleek pony tail. She was fresh-faced with no makeup except a pale pink lip gloss.

"I was just out by the dumpster getting rid of Aunt Christine's junk." She said this in a casual way, as if talking about taking out the garbage.

"Her junk? There must have been some mementos you wanted to keep to remember her by," I said.

"Yeah, a couple of photos when she and my dad were kids. But that's about it."

"Doesn't she have someone who might want some of her belongings?" I asked.

"No. Never married. No kids. My dad's gone, too. I was the

closest thing to family she had really." Amy took a can of furniture polish and a rag and, almost lovingly, ran it over the surfaces of the desk. Of course, the gesture did hardly more than move the gray residue, which had congealed with the polish to form mounds of black clumps, from the top of the desk to the floor.

She shook her head in frustration then began to pull items out of a carton on the floor and placed them on the desk. I recognized her glass dish with the pink paperclips and the high-heeled shoe tape dispenser. "This will have to do for now. I think this office will need a complete overhaul. I should insist the police come in to clean up their mess."

"I understand the funeral is set for Friday," I said. I wanted to refocus Amy's attention back to her aunt. The poor woman had only been gone a few days. Someone needed to think about her.

"Yeah. Can't wait to get that over with. We've got several exhibits planned over the next few months. New artists to bring on board. Contracts to draw up. Press releases. And of course a name change." She bent to pull something else out of the carton.

"Name change?"

Amy turned to me. "We certainly can't continue to call ourselves the Christine Dugan Gallery now, can we?"

Everything about this encounter was disturbing to me. "Amy, I just came by to pick up the check you said you had for me."

"Oh, yeah," she said. "I put it in the desk drawer here for safe keeping." She opened the drawer, extracted an envelope, and held it up to show me. The envelope was sealed and had my name carefully printed across the front. "This should be everything we owe you. After all, you completed the catering job as contracted. Not your fault what happened to Aunt Christine. Do you have an invoice for me?"

"Yes," I said, rooting around inside my purse to find it. "Wait a minute. I must have left it in my car. I'll be right back."

Leaving my purse behind, I scuttled out of her office and down the hall to the back door, which was still propped open. I'd left my car unlocked so opened the passenger seat and retrieved the folder with my invoice. As I closed the car door, a voice said, "Hello again."

I jumped and emitted a small squeal, then turned.

Rick was throwing a box into the dumpster. "Sorry, Trudie. Didn't mean to scare you." He shook his head, clapping the dust off his hands. "Cleaning out all the old stuff from my drawers and files is not an easy job."

"I guess not." I held up the folder to him. "Left my invoice in the car."

We both reached the door at the same time so that I was eye level with his chest, the sweaty t-shirt now clinging to his bulging abs.

Getting a whiff of his now musky scent, I swallowed hard.

Rick extended his hand and grinned. "After you, Madame," he said in an exaggerated French accent.

I stepped inside and dashed back down the hall, wondering how Julie Child had fared working side-by-side in hot kitchens with all male chefs when she'd taken classes at Le Cordon Bleu in Paris.

"Here it is," I said, handing Amy the folder.

She opened it to check the invoice then handed me the envelope with the check.

"Thank you," I said as I dropped it into my purse and turned to leave.

"Aren't you going to check to see if it's the right amount?"

"I trust you," I said, peering back over my shoulder and anxious to leave. If the check amount was wrong, I'd take care of it later. The whole vibe of this place was freaking me out. I should have taken Zach up on his offer to pick up the check or insisted Amy put it in the mail.

"One more thing, Trudie."

I turned, remembering that Amy had something she wanted to tell me.

She stood and glared at me. "I saw you the other night. Hiding in the alcove. Were you eavesdropping on our conversation with my aunt?"

My stomach jumped to my chest like a pancake flipped so high, its landing spot was uncertain. "I-I wasn't eavesdropping. I was only passing by from the ladies' room. I couldn't help but hear Christine talking to you and Rick."

"Then why were you hiding when we came out?" Amy asked.

"I wasn't hiding. I just didn't want you to feel embarrassed about what I'd overheard. That's all. It's really none of my business."

"No," she said, narrowing her eyes at me. "It's none of your business at all."

I turned and made my escape out into the alley. Once outside, I inhaled the fresh November air, only to get a whiff of garbage. Glancing at the dumpster just a few feet away from my car, I wondered why I hadn't seen Amy there when I'd pulled into the alley or why she hadn't passed me in the hallway as she hauled out her aunt's "junk."

I got into my car and turned on the ignition, then chose a low gear so I could ease my way down the steep driveway. The car began to move a little too quickly and I instinctively stepped on the brake pedal. It was loose and unresponsive. The car moved faster. I shifted into the lowest gear which did slow the vehicle down, but still continued its descent.

I thrust my foot onto the brake pedal again. Unresponsive. The car was moving too rapidly and would soon go careening into the busy traffic on Dupont Circle. Trying to think fast, I did the only thing I could think of. I slammed on the emergency brake.

My body flew forward, straining against the seatbelt, my head snapping forward and hitting the steering wheel. At the same time, the ungodly sound of screeching metal filled the air. My car came to an abrupt stop at the bottom of the driveway just inches from the traffic navigating the circle.

My heart pumped wildly as I exhaled a huge sigh of relief. I managed to retrieve my purse which had tumbled off the passenger seat onto the floor. I pulled out my cellphone and called Daniel to come and get me.

By the time I hung up the phone, Amy and Rick had reached me, frantic and wanting to help. Breathing hard, I lowered my window and turned to look at them wondering which one had just tried to kill me.

Chapter Eleven

The squad car arrived within ten minutes, lights flashing and sirens blaring, with Officer Billings at the wheel. It came to an abrupt stop directly in front of my car, and Daniel dashed out of the passenger seat, threw open my door, and wrapped his arms around me.

"Baby, are you okay?" he asked, now leaning back and holding me at arm's length to assess the damage.

"I-I think so. My head...." I touched the hardening bruise on my forehead and flipped the visor down to check it in the mirror. The knot seemed to be growing bigger by the minute, like a blueberry muffin peaking to the perfect height in the oven.

"We'll have to get you to the emergency room."

"I think I'm fine," I said.

But he was already on his radio, calling for help. "Let's make sure there's no concussion. Are you dizzy or nauseous?" he asked, not waiting for my answer.

Officer Billings exited the squad car, his face and posture all business as he approached Amy and Rick who had moved to the edge of the driveway to get out of the way. For once, I knew Will Billings was on my side, and I was grateful for it.

My body began to shudder like a martini in a cocktail shaker, and all I really wanted was to be in Daniel's arms. Before I knew it, however, an ambulance had pulled up in front of the police car followed by a tow truck, and I was being carted by EMTs into their waiting vehicle, with Daniel waving goodbye and letting me know he'd meet me at the hospital soon.

I LAY IN bed in a curtained cubicle in the ER after being examined by the doctor, who ascertained that I might have a mild concussion. All I knew was that my head felt like an overripe cantaloupe that had been sliced in half with my Santoku knife. They'd given me something for the pain and left me to rest.

I woke to someone calling my name. A woman's voice. I opened my eyes, but everything was blurred.

"Huh?" I asked. "Who's that?"

The woman stepped forward and came more into focus. "It's Deanna Carter," she said.

"Deanna? Who?"

She lowered herself into the chair by my bed. "Deanna. You remember, I'm sure. From the art gallery the other night."

I opened my eyes wider. Deanna. Yes, I remembered. The artist who crashed the party at the gallery and caused a scene. This woman had the same wild graying mane, the same desperate look in her eye.

At least today she wore a coat, a hand-knit garment with multicolored patterns resembling a Native American blanket.

"But, what…?" What was she doing here? I couldn't get out a complete sentence. How did she get into my room? Don't they screen visitors in the ER?

"I'm sure you're surprised to see me here out of the blue." She lowered her head and her shoulders began to shake, tears springing from her eyes. "I'm here to apologize," she managed to blurt out.

"Why? For causing a scene at the gallery?" But that was over and done days ago. Why here? Why now?

"No, not for that. Well yes, I do apologize for that night. But now, oh my god, I almost killed you." She sobbed harder. "I-I'm so, so sorry."

I scooted back and slowly sat myself up in the bed. "You mean today?" I asked. "You were the one who messed with my brakes?"

"Yes," she cried. "I didn't know it was your car. Honest to god, I thought it was Amy's."

"You were trying to kill Amy?" My vision kept clouding over, and I wondered when I was going to wake up from this bad dream.

"Well, no. Not exactly. I just wanted to scare her. I thought now that Christine was gone Amy would give me a chance to exhibit at the gallery. But she's as bad as her aunt. Worse. She said my art wasn't good enough or different enough to feature. She told me the schedule was full for the next six months anyway. That I should try other galleries."

I leaned forward, and the knife sliced through my melon head again. I put my hands up to try to hold it together then peered up at Deanna. "So you decided to cut her brakes?"

"Well, yes," she admitted, wiping her eyes. "I wanted to teach her a lesson, same as her aunt."

I gasped inwardly at the thought. Was Deanna the murderer? I shifted my gaze to the call button attached to the bed frame and wondered how I could press it without her knowing. Even if I couldn't, my curiosity got the best of me and I had to ask the question. "And how did you teach Christina a lesson?"

"You were there. You know what I did. I embarrassed her at the opening. In front of all her artsy friends and customers. Ha! Did you see her face when I pushed her? I showed her, didn't I?"

Over the past few months, I'd encountered my own share of disturbed individuals. One thing I had discovered the hard way was not to be confrontational but just to humor them. "I guess you did." Where in the world was Daniel already? He said he'd be here soon, but I didn't even know what time it was or how long I'd been here.

"Anyway," Deanna said. She gripped my hand in her long, icy fingers. "I just wanted to stop by to apologize. I never meant to hurt you, Trudie. Are you okay? Can you forgive me?"

"Yes, I'm fine." I squeezed her hand slightly to make her think I accepted her apology and then extracted my hand from hers. "Thanks for stopping by."

The gesture must have worked because she stood up. "Well then, I guess I'll be going." She gave me a quick smile and a wave and left.

I heaved a sigh and pressed the call button.

A hefty, graying nurse moved the curtain aside. "Yes? What can I help you with?"

"You can help me by monitoring who gets in here to see me," I said.

"Well, of course we do. One visitor at a time. That's the rule." She stepped into the room and pointed to a sign on the wall that said exactly that.

"I don't mean how many visitors. I mean who is allowed entrance to this room. A very disturbed woman was just in here when she shouldn't have been. She's the one who caused my accident. Didn't the police leave some kind of restrictions on visitors?"

The nurse paled. "Oh, my. Well, yes they did leave word about who could visit you. We had a medical emergency with the patient next door. I never saw anyone enter your room. I'm so sorry, Miss Fine."

"It's all right. Please, just contact Detective Daniel Goldman and tell him I need him to come as soon as possible."

When Daniel finally arrived, I filled him in about my surprise visitor.

"Deanna? The woman who caused the disturbance at the gallery? She's the one who cut your brakes?"

"Yes, but she thought it was Amy's car, not mine. She came to apologize."

"Apologize? She needs to be arrested for attempted murder, or at the very least, reckless endangerment." Daniel paced back and forth in the small curtained cubicle.

"But she told me she only meant to scare Amy, teach her a lesson.

I really don't think she intended to kill her." My head began to hurt as I followed Daniel's movements from one end of the room to the other.

He stopped. "That's just semantics. You cut someone's brakes, on an incline like that driveway, they're very likely going to get into a fatal accident, or at the very least, critically injured."

CUDDLED UNDER THE blankets at home that evening, I still couldn't seem to warm up. Every time I thought about that steep descent down the driveway, I began to shiver. Then I pictured Deanna at my bedside in the ER and began to shake even more.

"Here you go," Daniel said, delivering a steaming bowl of Mom's matzo ball soup, a leftover we'd had in the freezer. "The cure-all for whatever ails you." He set it on a tray table, plumped up my pillows so I could sit up, and then joined me in bed.

"Perfect," I said, giving him a kiss on the cheek. "Maybe this will warm me up." I sipped a spoonful of the delicious brew, sunk my spoon into a matzo ball, and savored the flavors. This was the height of comfort food, something I desperately needed right now.

I turned to Daniel. "So what's happened with Deanna?"

"She's been arrested, of course. Will said she wasn't surprised when they came to her door. But she confessed to cutting your brakes and went with them willingly."

"Poor Deanna," I said.

"Poor Deanna? You're lucky to be alive after what she did."

"I know. But she needs a psychiatrist, not jail time. I hope she can get help." I slurped another couple of spoonfuls of soup.

"Right now, she's being interrogated about the murder of Christine Dugan," he said.

I sat up straighter and shook my head. "But Deanna didn't kill Christine."

"How do you know?"

"Because she told me. Well, she didn't actually tell me that. But in Deanna's mind, she got back at Christine by storming the gallery and embarrassing her in front of the arts community."

Daniel laughed. "After all these years as a cop, why haven't I thought to believe the perpetrators who deny committing a crime? Here I've been spending hundreds of hours interrogating suspects to get the truth when all I had to do was ask them if they were guilty."

"Daniel, you know I don't mean it like that. She was disturbed enough to admit to cutting my brakes. Call it instinct or woman's intuition or whatever you want, but I'm sure she was not Christine's murderer."

He held out both hands in surrender. "Okay. I give up. You've made your point."

"Now tell me about my car. When can I get it back?" I asked.

"Lucky for you, Will has a neighbor who's a mechanic. He'll have it fixed sometime tomorrow."

"I guess Will has his good points, huh?" I said.

"He's a good man. Sometimes a little quick to judge, but he's got integrity. With more time, I think he's got a great future ahead of him. Glad to have him as my partner."

As I sipped another spoonful of goodness, Daniel brushed my hair out of my face with his fingers. I pulled his hand to my lips and kissed his palm. I realized that I'd stopped shivering and was beginning to warm up. "You know I'm the luckiest woman on earth right now to have you in my life."

"And I'm the luckiest man." He shook his head. "If I could only keep you out of trouble."

Chapter Twelve

O n Tuesday, Daniel dropped me off at work. Zach and I were prepping for a retirement dinner at a law firm on K Street. The senior partner was stepping down and moving to Palm Beach, Florida, which didn't sound like a step down to me.

The party was to be held in the executive suite on the top floor, and all twenty-five of the firm's lawyers were invited. They'd requested a very traditional dinner of Caesar salad, prime rib au jus, baked potatoes, and asparagus.

That afternoon, with the van packed, Zach and I made a stop at the U Street Coffee Shop to pick up fresh-baked French rolls and the retirement cake that Jennifer had made.

As usual, Jennifer, in her white chef's coat and pink paisley bandana, stood elbow-deep in flour, rolling out dough on the wooden work table.

Looking around the kitchen at the platters of breads, cakes, and pastries, I marveled at the amount of deliciousness this petite woman could turn out each day.

"Trudie, Zach," she said with a big smile. "I'd hug you guys, but you may not like that." She held out her arms white with flour, fingers gooey with dough.

"How's Rose doing?" Zach asked.

"She's taking her life back. Throwing herself into her sculpture. Trudie, we are both so appreciative of your help. Not just with Zeus and the agility competition, but Alan Bernstein is a gem of a lawyer. He's been keeping us both sane."

"I know. He's helped me out on more than one occasion. He has that calming effect on people." Alan had texted me that morning, in fact, trying to set a time to meet me for coffee. Busy preparing for tonight's catering job, I told him today was out of the question, but I finally agreed to meet him the next day at a Starbucks in Rockville not far from *A Fine Fix*. I'd put him off long enough and had no more excuses. If Daniel didn't approve of my meeting Alan for coffee then he'd just have to deal with it.

Zach loaded the rolls and cake into the van and waited while I walked up the block to my friend May's New Orleans-themed restaurant, *Maybelline's*. At the last minute, I had called to see if I could pick up a tray of her fabulous pralines to serve along with the cake at the retirement party that evening.

"Of course, sugah," May said in her syrupy voice. "You come on by and I'll load you up. Haven't seen you for a while. We'll have a nice visit."

Katie, May's hostess, met me at the door. I hadn't seen Katie since the summer. Now about six months pregnant, her bump had grown considerably, but she still looked like a little girl with her long red hair and freckled face.

"Trudie, it's so good to see you." We hugged, her belly holding me back a little.

Ready for the dinner crowd, she wore a black tunic embroidered with the *Maybelline's* logo over black leggings and flats. She seemed to glow with this pregnancy despite the fact that the baby's father, May's brother, had died so tragically.

Katie escorted me into the kitchen where May was boxing up the pralines. She stood tall and regal, wearing one of her signature kaftans, this one a swirl of purples and golds.

"*Ma cherie*," May said, holding out her arms to me.

I hugged her, as usual surprised by her thin frame. "May, how are you? I've heard nothing but fabulous success stories since you reopened. Four stars from every critic."

"Yes, but I can't take the credit. Chef Marcel has captured N'awlins with his Cajun French flavors he brings to each dish. He's a Loosiana native, you know. We're goin' to take DC by storm on Thursday with our Thanksgivin' special menu. Maybe you and Daniel would like to come partake, shugah."

"Would have loved that, but Mom is whipping up a feast that day."

"May," Katie said. "You're going to be so busy that night. I wish you'd let me work. Honestly, I'll be fine."

"Katie, I don't want you on your feet so much. It's not good for you or the baby. Just look at those ankles."

The three of us peered down at Katie's feet. The few inches of flesh that showed between her leggings and her flats were slightly puffy, but nothing near as swollen as mine looked after a busy event on my feet.

"I'll wear compression hose, if that makes you feel better. Let me help you out for Thanksgiving."

"Uh-uh," May said, shaking her head. She shook a long, thin finger at Katie. "You go have a nice little family dinner with your parents. You told me yourself that they are tryin' to reestablish a relationship with you."

"My parents will be out of town. They're going to some spa in Arizona. I don't remember the last time they stayed home for Thanksgiving."

"Katie," I said. "Mom would absolutely love it if you'd come have Thanksgiving with us. She goes bonkers over pregnancies and babies. It would make her day."

"I don't know. I love your mom, but it would be an imposition." Katie turned to May and put her hands on her hips. "And I really want to work that day."

"No, ma'am," May said. "It's settled. You're having Thanksgiving with Trudie at her mom's house."

THE RETIREMENT DINNER was a great success. Of course, with highball glasses filled and refilled with Glenfiddich, TV dinners would have been well-received by the guests. Many, however, raved about the food and asked for our business cards, which I always kept handy in my apron pocket.

In the morning, after picking up my car from the mechanic, I met Zach at work to help empty the van and prepare for the next gig. We sat on either side of the desk, finalizing the list for our catering job that night, a Turkey Trot dance at a local senior center. This event, a tradition for the past twenty years, had used the same caterer and the same menu every year. But with the caterer now retired and closed down, we had been offered a trial run. The menu, we were told by the center's activity director, must be traditional Thanksgiving fare for the seniors, most of whom didn't have families to dine with on the actual holiday.

Zach and I had balked a little at this. We could provide the usual Thanksgiving fare, but had lots of ideas for elevating the food at this event.

"This is your opportunity to make some new traditions," Zach suggested to the director. "New caterer, new menu."

"And this is your opportunity," the well-seasoned director said, "To show us you can deliver what we're used to. Remember, this is just a tryout. We can always go with someone else next year."

"All right," I said, hoping for some kind of negotiation. "What if we included all the traditional foods, turkey, stuffing, sweet potatoes, green beans, pumpkin pie, but added a few of our own unique dishes?"

Smoothing his salt and pepper mustache between his fingers, the man considered this a moment then finally agreed. "As long as the expected dishes are served, I guess a few new ones wouldn't be a problem."

I KEPT CHECKING my watch, feeling jittery about my meeting with Alan. I'd planned to tell Daniel about my coffee date, but just couldn't figure out how without upsetting him. I supposed what Daniel didn't know wouldn't hurt him. On the other hand, our relationship had reached the point of complete honesty. Well, I hadn't been dishonest. I'd just neglected to mention it to him.

I'd taken a good deal of time that morning getting ready, choosing not to wear my usual headband in my dark brown shoulder-length hair. And I'd gone through half my wardrobe until I decided on a forest green, long-sleeved knit dress with a navy and green scarf and tall brown boots.

It wasn't that I wanted to pursue a relationship with Alan. Daniel was my one and only love. It's just that I hadn't seen Alan in so long and, like any other woman, wanted to look attractive. Well, these are the things I kept telling myself anyway.

Starbucks adjoined a large book store on Rockville Pike. Seating space was minimal, but the clientele here tended to focus on their reading material or electronic devices. That provided the comfort of going unnoticed.

Alan had already secured a table by the window with comfortable cushioned chairs. He stood and greeted me with that big, warm smile of his, taking both my hands in his. "Trudie, you look great."

"So do you," I said. Alan, like most successful lawyers, had a bevy of custom suits made of the finest fabrics. He wore expensive silk ties and Italian leather shoes.

"I took the liberty of ordering you a skim caramel macchiato, no whip. I remembered from last time. Is that okay?"

Really? That was a good four months ago. "Sure. That's exactly what I would have ordered," I said.

He leaned in toward me and put a hand on mine. "I've missed you, Trudie. So glad you called me the other day."

"Yes. Thank you again for taking on Rose's case. It's been a great relief for my friend Jennifer."

"That's my job. Thank you for the referral. And how have you been? Is your business doing well?"

That hit my soft spot and I smiled. "Zach and I are doing very well. Lots of business. And Jennifer is doing all our baking now. We catered our first large-scale wedding the other day. I think we've got a foot in the door with several different wedding planners." I took a sip of my coffee and waited, not sure where our conversation was going.

Alan sat back in his seat, coffee in hand, his eyes lasered on mine. "And you're still with Detective Goldman?" he asked.

"Yes, we're still together."

He exhaled and his smile withered, deflating like a failed soufflé just out of the oven.

I looked down and picked a piece of lint from my sleeve. This was definitely awkward. Alan was a great guy and a good friend who I'd avoided to spare Daniel's feelings. But didn't I have the right to choose my own friends? Daniel, in fact, had continued occasional lunches with his co-worker, Sergeant Sherrie Flowers, who had tried on more than one occasion to get her hooks into him. He'd been honest with me about those meetings and I trusted him. Now it was Daniel's turn to trust me. But was I being truthful with myself? Did I have feelings for Alan? Or was I just flattered that an attractive, successful attorney was enamored with me?

I smiled at Alan. "Okay. So you remembered my favorite Starbucks drink. What's yours? Next time, if I get here first I want to be able to place the order."

His face brightened. "I'm a pretty straight-forward Starbucks customer. Just a simple grande triple skinny vanilla soy latte is all I need. Sometimes a cinnamon scone."

"Uh, next time I'll just wait for you."

He laughed and we settled back in our chairs.

"You've had a bit of a harrowing week, haven't you?" he asked, his smile gone.

"That's one way to describe it." I knew he was referring to Christine's murder. I would have liked to talk to him about it, but how much could I tell? Alan was Rose's defense lawyer. Daniel and Will were investigators on the case. I'd have to be as objective as possible, something that would be difficult for me. I wondered if he knew about the incident with my car the day before.

I decided to stick with neutral territory. "The craziest part of the week was participating with Rose's dog Zeus in an agility competition."

"What?"

Okay. Something he didn't know about. I went into great detail about my experience in the agility ring and soon had Alan laughing again.

"Trudie, how do you get yourself into these situations?" he asked.

"That's exactly what Daniel wants to know." I took a sip of my coffee.

Alan glanced out the window and then back at me. "I suppose that's why we love you."

What? I choked on my drink and sprayed a whole mouthful of caramel macchiato onto Alan's jacket, shirt and tie.

"Oh no. Not again." I grabbed a handful of napkins and dabbed at his stained clothing, with little effect.

Alan put his head back and laughed. Then I started laughing along with him remembering how I had ruined his silk tie with my coffee the first time we'd met.

Chapter Thirteen

Back in our warehouse kitchen with Zach, he already had two large turkeys roasting in the oven along with several sweet potatoes for a casserole and a couple of butternut squash to transform into a creamy soup.

Jennifer would supply us with several dozen sweet potato biscuits along with pumpkin chiffon and pecan pies, and a few dozen apple strudels.

"Hey, Zach. What are you doing for Thanksgiving this year?" I asked as I added fresh cranberries and sugar to a pot of boiling water. Zach's parents had moved to an over fifty-five gated community in Florida a couple of years before. "You're welcome to come to Mom's. She'd be ecstatic to see you."

Zach was sautéing chopped onions and celery, softening the vegetables enough to add to his mushroom and chestnut dressing. "Thanks, Trudie. I would love to come, but I'm helping Ally out that day in her restaurant. Reservations have been pouring in. She's gotten great reviews since opening last week. People are really curious about her healthy take on comfort food."

"I'm glad to hear that." I hesitated a moment as I chopped apples and walnuts and zested an orange while waiting for the cranberries to pop. Then I glanced up at Zach. "And how are the two of you progressing? As a couple, I mean?" I'd been more than a little worried. Over the years, Ally had often taken advantage of Zach's feelings for her, used him for whatever she needed at the time, chewed him up and then spit him out. Was she stringing him along again so he would help get her new restaurant going?

"We're progressing, but definitely taking it step-by-step."

I had seen a difference in them, first at her restaurant opening and then at the agility competition. They seemed more comfortable together.

I just hoped history wouldn't repeat itself.

At four o'clock, with the van loaded, Zach headed over to the senior center while I stopped at Jennifer's house to pick up the baked goods for the event. Jennifer did her baking at the U Street Coffee Shop early each morning and worked until two-thirty after most of the lunch crowd were gone.

At work in the coffee shop, Jennifer, although petite, looked a little intimidating proofing the dough, rolling it out and taking command of her ovens. But that afternoon, when she opened her front door dressed in jeans and a pink turtleneck shirt, I warmed immediately to her welcoming smile.

"Hi, Trudie. I've got everything boxed up and ready for you. Come on in." As she led me to the kitchen, her brown pixie cut, spiked at the crown, seemed to react to every move, giving her a spritely air.

I'd been prepared for an onslaught from Zeus, and looking around, I realized I missed him.

Jennifer noticed my forlorn look and laughed. "Zeus is in the barn with Rose. Do you want me to get him?"

"No, I have to get over to the venue to help Zach set up."

Several boxes of baked goods sat on the kitchen table. "I'll get my coat and help you load your car," Jennifer said.

"How is the case going?" I asked as we made the first of two trips to the car.

"It will take a while to get a court date. In the meantime, we're hoping they find the real murderer." Jennifer stacked the boxes neatly in my trunk then stood up and put her hand on my arm. "I heard what happened to you at the gallery the other day. Are you okay? And what were you doing there anyway?"

My hand instinctively went up to the bruise on my forehead. The swelling had gone down a bit and I'd been able to cover the blue with concealer, but it still hurt to the touch. "I'm doing okay. A little creeped out by the experience. I went to the gallery because Amy had called me to pick up the money she still owed us."

"She paid you?" Jennifer asked. "Rose is still waiting for her share of the artwork that was sold. She can't even pin Amy down to the items that were purchased that night. Rose wants to go over there and see for herself which pieces are gone and those that sold. But the judge instructed her to stay away from the gallery."

"What about you?" I asked. "Maybe you can speak to Amy in

person."

Jennifer shivered. "Not sure I could go back to that place. I still have nightmares about it."

"I don't blame you," I said, cringing at the thought of ever revisiting the Christine Dugan Gallery. "What if someone went with you?"

"I don't know anyone who I could even ask. And I'd feel pretty vulnerable walking into that place. Rose may just have to wait the six weeks until the exhibit items are returned to find out what was sold."

A thought occurred to me. "What if you took Zeus along? He's a pretty good judge of character. He'd protect you."

"Hmm, maybe," Jennifer said. "Let me think about it. Rose really does need the money to pay her attorney's fees, and I'd love to get it for her."

With all the baked goods loaded in my trunk, I headed for the senior center.

In the past several days, Zach and I had catered an upscale art exhibit, a glittering wedding at an historic estate, and a retirement dinner for a group of stuffy, rich business men.

But the Turkey Trot dinner dance at the senior center turned out to be our favorite by far. The rec center had been decorated with paper turkeys and cornucopia, orange, yellow, and brown crepe paper streamers, gourds, pumpkins, and haystacks with scarecrows.

Several long tables along both sides and the back of the room were set with Thanksgiving-themed paper cloths, napkins, plates, and plastic cutlery. Matching hot and cold cups accompanied serve-yourself urns of hot apple cider and coffee along with water, sodas and ice.

The tables in the front held our Thanksgiving fare served buffet-style in platters and chafing dishes. We'd elevated each dish enough so that while looking and tasting traditional, there was just a bit extra that kept the guests coming back for more. A corn pudding that Zach had whipped up at the last minute was the biggest hit of all.

The DJ who often entertained at the center was set up in one corner, and most of the seniors danced the night away, some accompanied by walkers and wheelchairs. They shouted out song requests for their favorite big band music from the thirties and forties, and the DJ complied.

On such a festive occasion, I wore my orange apron with *A Fine Fix* stitched in purple across the breast pocket. Zach wore a purple long-sleeved shirt with the logo in orange. A few of the women alternately pulled him onto the dance floor for a slow dance, and we were both coaxed out to join a Conga line. At the end of the evening, we were given official status as members of the senior center.

At ten, I arrived home and pulled into the driveway. My adrenaline was running high as always after a successful event, and I looked forward to a couple of days rest before our next gig set for Saturday. The house was dark, as expected, because Daniel was working late so he could take off the next day for the Thanksgiving holiday. With the porch light out, I fumbled to find the right key and get it into the lock.

Something rustled through the dry leaves on the front lawn. Deer, most likely. Often families of deer from a nearby park hung out in the neighborhood, seemingly oblivious to human comings and goings.

By the size of it in my hand, I was sure I had the correct key, and jiggling it to try to fit into the lock. I turned the key upside-down, still with no success. I heard the rustling sound again, getting closer. Something, or someone, was approaching me. Still attempting to unlock the door, I turned to look over my shoulder. The darkness took shape, and I wasn't sure if I was looking at a tree, an animal, or a human being.

Finally, the key slid into the lock and I turned the knob. I slipped into the house quickly, slammed the door shut, and locked it. Inside the darkness of the foyer, I leaned back against the door, breathing hard. Then I ran my hand along the wall to locate the light switch, flipped it on, and gasped.

A clown doll with a cord around its neck swung back and forth in front of me, its hair made from looped red yarn topped by a pointed purple, satin hat. The cord was attached to the light fixture above. The clown's porcelain head lolled to one side, its eyes open wide and its mouth gaped in horror, his porcelain hands and feet splayed as if asking for mercy. Hanging from his neck was a miniature duplicate of the spiral pendant that had killed Christine, and pinned to the doll's clothing was a piece of paper. For a moment, I froze, unable to move. Then with a shaking hand, I reached out and, extracting the push pin, took hold of the paper. It was folded in quarters, so I opened it once and then a second time. Written in what appeared to be a red Sharpie, it said, "You told!"

I dropped the note on the floor, and for the first time, it occurred to me that whoever hung the clown might still be in the house.

My instinct was to run out of the house, get back in my car, and drive as far away as I could. But what if the rustling I'd heard outside was someone waiting for me to do just that very thing?

I gazed up at the clown doll, still swinging back and forth in front of me. I couldn't move. Didn't want to move. If the intruder was in the house, I didn't want to be the one to find him—or her. I sunk to the floor and eased my cellphone from my purse. Only twenty-two percent left on the battery. It was enough. I'd intended to recharge my device tonight while I slept. For now, I'd have to use the phone wisely.

I found Daniel's name on the screen and touched it. The phone rang once, twice, three times. Answer the phone, Daniel. Answer the phone. His voice mail message came on. He was out of the office or away from his desk. "Please leave a message and I'll get back to you," his voice said. I would leave a message, but when would he listen to it?

At the tone, I hissed, "Daniel, come home now. Help. I need you. We had an intruder."

Now what? Who else could I call?

I dialed 9-1-1.

"Emergency fire and rescue," the woman answered.

"Help. I've had an intruder," I whispered and gave her the address.

"Is the intruder still in your home?" she asked.

"I'm not sure. Please, come quick. I'm scared."

"We have a squad car on the way now. Where are you?"

"I'm in the foyer. I'm afraid to go any further into the house."

"All right. Stay in place. See if there's a place to hide nearby. Do you want me to remain on this call?"

"Yes, but my phone may lose power."

"Don't worry. Help will be there before that happens. Now see where you can hide."

Across from the door was a coat closet. If I scooted across the floor, I could duck inside. I cringed at the thought of getting closer to the hanging doll but quietly eased myself over to the closet. I reached up and gently turned the knob, but stopped. What if the intruder was hiding in the closet? It's possible that he—or she—planned to enter the house, hang the doll, and leave as quickly as possible. But what if I arrived before that? Where would the intruder hide, hoping for an easy get-away? In the coat closet, of course.

I took my hand off the knob and backed away.

"No place to hide," I whispered into the phone.

"Okay," she said. "Just hunker down. They'll be there any minute."

On the floor, I leaned my back against the door. Something above me rattled. I peered up. The front door knob was moving. Someone was turning it back and forth, trying to get in. I scooted away from the door and covered my mouth to keep myself from screaming.

I heard a key jiggling in the lock. The knob turned.

Oh no, oh no, oh no.

Quietly, the door opened and Daniel stood there looking down at me. Yes, Daniel was here. I exhaled my breath and started to talk, but he put his finger to his lips and silently entered the house, gun in hand. He must have gotten my message.

He peered quizzically at the hanging doll. Then he began to check the house, first the coat closet then room by room, flicking on the light before entering each one. Moments later, sirens approached. I stood just as the door opened and a uniformed cop entered. I could see the squad car lights flashing at the bottom of the driveway.

"I think it's okay," I said. "Detective Daniel Goldman is here. He lives here, in fact. He just came home, and he's checking the house."

"Are you all right, miss?" he asked.

"Yes, but this thing scared the shitake out of me." I nodded toward the hanging clown.

Daniel came back into the foyer. "The house is clear," he said.

"We've got someone checking the back yard. Nothing yet, sir."

"They left a note," I said, pointing to the floor.

"Trudie, you touched it?"

"Of course I touched it. How else could I read it?"

He went to the kitchen and returned with a plastic sandwich bag and used it to pick up the note. Then he flipped it inside out so the note was inside.

"You told!" Daniel read through the bag. "What does that mean?" He looked at me.

"I'm not sure. Maybe it has to do with what I told Will Billings about Amy and Rick. Or maybe that I told about Deanna cutting the brakes."

"Or maybe what you told Will about Rose and Christine's argument," Daniel added. He handed the bag to the policeman. "Take this down to the station. And let's get this thing down," he said, glancing up at the clown doll. "See if we can get some prints in here."

I heard a woman's voice coming from somewhere and peered down at my phone. "Oh. I forgot. Hello," I said, putting the phone to my ear. "Are you still there?"

"Yes." The woman on the other end laughed. "I'm still here. It sounds as if everything's okay now, right?"

"Right," I said. "Can I ask your name?"

"Melinda," she said.

"Thank you, Melinda."

"That's what I'm here for."

DANIEL AND I sat cuddled on the sofa with a fleece throw and a bottle of Sauvignon Blanc. He rubbed my arms up and down to help me stop shivering.

"What do you think that clown doll meant?" I asked him. "Do you think it was a threat?"

"I don't know. It might just be an attempt to scare you."

"Well they were pretty successful at that," I said. "That note could have come from Amy or Rick. I did tell Will about the confrontation with Christine that I'd overheard. But how would they know unless Will questioned them about it?" I looked up at Daniel. "Did he?"

"He did speak to them after your incident with the car."

"What about Deanna? She confessed to me that she'd cut my brakes because she thought it was Amy's car. Of course, I reported the incident, and she was arrested that same day. If she's been out on bail, maybe it was her." I turned to lean my back against Daniel and stretched my legs out on the sofa.

He put his arm around me and kissed the top of my head. "There's something else you told Will. About Rose and Christine and their argument about her contract. Remember? That's what led to Rose's arrest."

"I know, but somehow I don't think Rose would have done something like that. If it was her, why would she put that pendant on the clown? Why would she give herself away?"

Daniel shrugged. "Or, maybe she thought the pendant would naturally point to someone else because we would assume she would never do such a thing."

I shivered again and hugged my body, snuggling against Daniel's warmth. "I don't know. I don't want to think about it anymore. I'll leave it up to the police to figure it out."

"Well, that's refreshing coming from Trudie Fine, the master at cooking up schemes to catch the criminal element in our Nation's Capital."

I punched him in the arm. "Daniel. Don't make fun of me. I'm really spooked."

"I know, baby. Hopefully we'll be able pick up some prints to identify the intruder. But it may take a while."

I turned my face toward Daniel. "In the meantime, I don't ever want to come home alone at night again."

"We won't let that happen," he said into my hair. "Now other than this intruder episode, how was your day?" Daniel asked as he tucked the corners of the blanket securely around me.

I guessed this was my opening to tell him about Alan. I took a sip of the wine, stalling while trying to find a way to start. I told Daniel about the Turkey Trot dance and how much fun Zach and I had with the seniors.

"I know what you mean. I've done some security side jobs at a couple of senior facilities.

Once you get talking to the older generation, you realize what rich, vibrant lives they've led and how much wisdom they have to impart."

"Well we blew them away with our food. They want us to come back next year." I took another nonchalant sip of wine and then blurted, "Oh, did I mention that I had coffee with Alan Bernstein today?"

Daniel reddened and began to choke on his wine. "Bernstein? No, you didn't mention it. What were you doing with him?"

"He wanted to thank me for referring Rose to him, wanted to catch up, see how I was doing." I poured myself another glass of wine and waited for Daniel's next reply.

"He could easily have thanked you, and found out how you were doing, over the phone."

"Yes, that's true." The thought of Sergeant Sherrie Flowers again emboldened me, and I lifted my chin. "Daniel, I think of Alan as a friend. He's helped Zach, he's helped May, and now he's helping Rose. He's a good guy. So if I want to get together with him occasionally for coffee, then I will."

Daniel absent-mindedly twirled a piece of my hair around his finger then shook his head. "It's just that you know and I know Bernstein has a thing for you. And it makes me a little crazy to think of you meeting him for coffee."

"And how do you think I feel when you have lunch with Sergeant Flowers?"

"That's different. Sherrie is a colleague. We're discussing business."

"It's no different than my meeting Alan for coffee. You and Sherrie," and I said her name with extra emphasis, "can darn well discuss business in the office. We both know she has a thing for you and won't stop trying."

Daniel leaned his head back on the sofa, his eyes on mine. "But I don't want Sherrie Flowers. I only want you."

I picked up my glass of wine and took a sip, all the while gazing back at him. "And I don't want Alan Bernstein. I only want you."

Still holding his glass, Daniel stood and pulled me to my feet. "I think we need to continue this discussion in the bedroom."

I grabbed the bottle and said, "I think that's a good idea."

Chapter Fourteen

Waking up on Thanksgiving morning, Daniel and I luxuriated in bed.

"You know what I miss?" he said. "The smell of a turkey cooking on Thanksgiving morning and the sound of marching bands in the Macy's Day Parade. My mom loved the parade. She used to watch the whole thing while she cooked our Thanksgiving dinner, from the Snoopy balloon to the Rockettes kicking up their heels in front of Macy's to Santa on his sleigh."

"Did you watch the parade, too?"

"Nah, I'd hear it, though. It seeped through the walls of our apartment all morning until it was time for the football games on TV. That was what Dad and I liked to do, if he didn't have to work that day. For cops, sometimes the holidays are the busiest days of the year. And Philly was no different than DC."

"You know," I said. "This is our first Thanksgiving together. We need to make our own traditions." I leaned over Daniel and retrieved the remote from his bedside table, kissing him on the way back to my side of the bed. I clicked on the TV and tuned into the parade, then got up and headed out of the bedroom.

"Hey, where are you going?" he asked.

"To get some breakfast. I'll be back."

I returned about twenty minutes later with a tray of coffee, eggs and English muffins. We plumped our pillows against the headboard and ate while we watched the floats, marching bands and huge balloons.

"I think I could get used to this," Daniel said. He pulled me closer and kissed my forehead.

"Me, too."

ALL MY FAVORITE traditions merged into one when we arrived at my parents' house. The smells of roasted turkey and pumpkin pie, the football game broadcasting from the TV, the flaming logs crackling in the fireplace.

Daniel and I had picked up Katie. I knew Mom would be thrilled beyond words to see her. "Mom, you remember Katie, May's hostess at her restaurant."

"So nice to see you again, Mrs. Fine. I brought these for you. Hope you like them." Katie held out a bouquet of autumn flowers that she'd insisted we stop to get on our way here.

"They're lovely. Thank you, dear. And please, call me Helen." My mother engulfed her in a maternal hug then stood back, holding Katie by the shoulders. "Just look at you. Are you what, five, maybe six months along? You'll have to tell me all about it."

"Six months." Katie's translucent complexion seemed even paler next to the bold rusts, golds, and burgundies of the bouquet. In her white tunic shirt over maternity jeans and baby pink Keds, she seemed diminished by Mom's fully coiffed blonde hair and turquoise print pant suit.

Daniel hugged my mother and went into the kitchen to fetch a beer from the fridge before joining Dad on the sofa in front of the TV. I loved the way he felt so comfortable in my parents' house. They had welcomed him like family, and he had accepted the status easily.

Mom went to put the flowers in a vase, and I brought Katie into the family room to meet Dad.

"I'm going to see if Mom needs help in the kitchen. Want to come?" I asked Katie after making the introductions.

"If you don't mind, I'd like to watch the game. I love football." Then, as if she'd lived in my parents' house for years, she plopped down on the love seat adjacent to the sofa where Daniel and my dad sat, each on one end. Before I knew it, the three of them were yelling at the TV, objecting to the referee's calls.

"Need some help?" I asked Mom when I entered the kitchen.

"Sure. You can put out the *hors d'eourves*."

On the counter sat a virtual feast: a hollowed-out pumpernickel bread with spinach dip, a plate of salmon spread with crackers, and a huge platter of crudités, cheeses and olives.

"Mom, we're not going to have any room for dinner."

She kissed me on the forehead. "Dinner isn't for two hours, sweetheart. Your friends shouldn't go hungry."

"I guarantee they won't."

Before we brought the food out, I filled her in about Katie's situation and how she was living at May's house until the baby was born, possibly longer. With the baby's father deceased, Katie needed all the support she could get.

Mom pulled out plates and napkins while I set the *hors d'oeuvres* on serving trays. "Oh, and Mom, I forgot to tell you that Daniel and I invited his new partner to dinner. He had no place to go, and we knew you wouldn't mind."

"Of course I don't mind. The more, the merrier."

As if on cue, the doorbell rang. Daniel and I reached the foyer at the same time to open the door. Mom followed close behind.

"Will, so glad you could make it," Daniel said, shaking his hand and patting him on the back.

"Mom," I said, "This is Bill—I mean Will Billings. So sorry, Will. I do that every time."

"That's okay," he said. "I had friends growing up who called me Bill. Actually, they called me Billy Billings because they liked the way it sounded. So you're welcome to call me either, Will or Bill, or even Billy. I'm just getting used to calling you Trudie, so we're even." Will smiled, revealing a dimple on his left cheek, none on the right. The first thing I'd seen about him that wasn't perfect. Even today, dressed casually in a black and purple Western Illinois University sweatshirt, his dark-wash jeans sported a sharp crease down each leg, and his sneakers were an unblemished white.

"I'm Helen," my mom said and drew him in for a hug.

"Welcome."

Will stood awkwardly and seemed not sure where to put his hands. Obviously not used to hugs.

"Go on into the family room and introduce yourself, Will," Daniel said. "I'll get you a beer."

"That's okay," I said. "I'll get the beer. Mom and I have to bring out the *hors d'eourves* anyway."

"And I've got some nice herbal iced tea for Katie," Mom said.

In the family room, Will had taken a seat next to Katie. I squeezed in alongside Daniel, and my mother sat in an armchair. The halftime show had come on and Dad went over to the fireplace to add another log.

"Well, this is cozy, isn't it?" Mom asked. "Will, how long have you been in the area?"

"Just since the summer." All eyes were directed at him, and he shifted in his seat. "I'm from a small town in Illinois, far enough from Chicago that there wasn't much going on in the police department. Thought I'd go someplace with more action."

"Well, there's plenty of action here," my dad said. "Right, Daniel? A few murders even Trudie's had to deal with. That woman at the art gallery last week, Mel Schwartz back in July, and that poor kid, you know, at May's restaurant."

Katie dipped her head to her lap.

"Sid," Mom said. "Let's not bring up all that unpleasantness."

"It's okay," Katie said. "I don't mind."

"Don't mind what?" Dad asked, looking back and forth from

Katie to my mother to me.

"That was May's brother, Micah, who was killed." Katie spoke quietly, her hand resting on her belly. "My baby's father."

Dad shook his head. "I'm sorry, young lady. I didn't intend to bring up a painful subject like that. Damned shame."

"Sid." Mom huffed a sigh.

"It's okay," Katie said again. "Really."

"I remember that." Will nodded. "First case on the job here." He looked more closely at Katie and seemed to have an epiphany. "I remember you, too. Didn't know you were uh…."

"No. Most people don't know I'm having Micah's baby." Then she looked around at all of us in the awkward silence. "Of course, they might realize it after the baby's born. He probably won't look like me." She smiled shyly at her own joke.

I hadn't really thought about Micah's being black since finding out about the pregnancy. I suppose it had been on Katie's mind quite a bit, especially with parents who were still attempting to talk her into putting the baby up for adoption.

"So you're having a boy?" Mom asked. "How wonderful. Well, if you're in the market for a baby sitter, look no further. Sid and I would love to watch him now and then."

Katie smiled. "Thank you, Mrs. Fine. That's very kind of you."

"Helen," my mother corrected.

"Thank you, Helen."

"After all, we'll need to get some practice for when we're grandparents one day, right Trudie?"

I felt my face redden. "Mom."

Daniel chuckled and elbowed me. "Absolutely right, Helen."

I glanced at him. We hadn't spoken at all about children. Hadn't even gotten to the subject of marriage, only intimations of what our life could, or would, be like together. And for the second time in a week, my future bubbled up in front of me like an effervescent soda.

Halftime was over, and Katie, Dad, and Daniel resumed their banter with the TV. Will leaned forward and joined in with just as much animation. "What? Do you believe that call? Is that ref blind?"

The doorbell rang.

My mother jumped up from her seat. "That must be Mr. Bernstein."

Oh no, I thought, remembering the time last summer when Daniel and Alan both sat at mom's dinner table together. It hadn't gone well.

"Alan Bernstein?" Daniel directed an accusing glance my way. "What's he doing here?

I shrugged my ignorance.

"I invited him, of course," Mom said, heading for the door. "I didn't think he had a place to go for the holiday, so I called him this morning."

"Bernstein?" Will said. "Rose Mendez's lawyer?"

Daniel put his hands to his face and shook his head. "One and the same. This isn't the first time he's nosed his way in here."

Alan grinned amiably as he entered the family room. "Hi, all. Great, you've got the game on."

"Sid, bring in another chair. Alan, please sit." She pointed to the place where Dad had been sitting, right next to me.

Alan didn't hesitate, took the seat and nodded at me. "Trudie."

I gave him a wan smile. "Hello, Alan."

Then leaning forward, Alan said, "Detective Goldman."

Daniel nodded to him, stone-faced. "Alan." He put his arm around me and pulled me closer.

"Alan," I said. "You know Katie, and this is Will Billings."

Will still had his mouth open at the surprise of sharing the evening with Rose's defense attorney. But he held out his hand to Alan. "Mr. Bernstein."

"Officer Billings? Correct?" Alan asked, shaking his hand. "I've seen you in court."

"That's right," Daniel said. "And you'll see him in court again soon as we proceed with this case."

Like the referees on TV, I signaled a time out. "Hey, it's Thanksgiving. No shop talk today, okay?"

Everyone turned their attention back to the TV, but an awkward silence replaced the previous lively interchange until Mom finally announced that dinner was ready.

At dinner, Mom had me seated between Daniel and Alan on one side of the table with Katie and Will on the other. My parents each sat on an end.

Daniel had moved his chair closer to mine and ate only with his right hand while keeping his left hand solidly on my leg, thereby marking his territory. He looked past me at Alan. "I understand you and Trudie met for coffee yesterday?"

Alan's eyebrows lifted, as if surprised that I'd told Daniel about it. "Yes. It was great to see her. We had a good laugh, didn't we Trudie?" He grinned at me and, feeling my face flush, I turned my attention to my plate, capturing some of the gooey, melted marshmallows from the sweet potato casserole with my fork.

"What about?" Daniel asked.

"I-I was telling him about my experience with Zeus in the agility ring. Or inexperience, I should say."

"Tell us about it," Katie said. "I had a friend who was really into agility training with her dog. I used to go and watch them."

"Yes, tell us," Mom said.

I related the story without mentioning Rose's name, but did imply that I was filling in for a friend. By the end of the story, I had everyone laughing, even Daniel.

"So how is that murder case going, Daniel?" Dad asked. "I heard you made an arrest."

Will, a forkful of mashed potatoes midway to his mouth, peered up at Daniel.

Daniel took a sip of his beer and swallowed. "That's right. Can't really talk about it though, Sid. The defense attorney is sitting at this table."

All eyes moved to Alan and he nodded, slicing a piece of turkey with his knife and fork. He smiled. "I sure am."

"Oh, my." Mom put her hand to her mouth. "I'm so sorry. When I invited you, Alan, I didn't realize..."

"Not a problem at all, Helen. We're all civilized folks sitting around your bounteous Thanksgiving table. We'll just move the conversation in another direction." He dipped the piece of turkey into the pool of gravy on his plate, put it in his mouth, and chewed with a big grin on his face.

Dad persisted. "So if you've made an arrest, I guess the case is solved. Right, Will?"

Will's eyes widened. I could see his conflict about whether to be polite to my father and answer the question or try to deflect it in some way. He glanced at Daniel who was busily partaking of his dinner, trying to ignore the conversation. Daniel's face was red and the vein in his temple bulged.

"Sid," my mother said. "Alan said we should change the subject."

Will put his knife and fork down on the plate and turned to Dad. "I will say, Mr. Fine, no case is open and shut. Yes, we did make an arrest based on evidence we had at the time. But as investigators, we need to continue to look at every piece of evidence and every possible suspect."

"I'll drink to that." Alan tipped his wine glass toward Will then took a sip.

Daniel shook his head but didn't look up. By the pressure of his hand on my knee, I could sense his rising anger. I turned to him and pushed his hand off.

He frowned at me. "What?"

I spoke quietly. "You were squeezing too hard. It hurt."

Daniel's eyes softened. "Sorry. I didn't realize—"

"Trudie, is that man abusing you?" Alan asked, sounding serious but with a twinkle in his eye. "Want to get a restraining order? I can help."

"Bernstein, do you have to make light of everything?" I almost expected smoke to come out of Daniel's ears with this comment.

"There's nothing light about physical abuse," Alan said.

Daniel dropped his fork on his plate with a loud clang. "I've had just about enough of him."

"Daniel." I put my hand on his arm. "Calm down. This is a family dinner."

"Yeah? And whose family does he belong to?" Daniel stood and threw his napkin on the table then walked into the other room.

"I'm sorry," I said to everyone then followed after him.

Daniel gazed out the sliding glass doors that led from the family room onto the patio. An outside light fixture illuminated the flagstone patio on which sat a barbeque grill, a round glass table, and chairs. Beyond that was only darkness.

Standing next to him, I put my arm around his waist and my head on his shoulder. Our reflections stared back at us, Daniel several inches taller, and me a bit wider, but still a comfortable fit. I tilted my head up to him. "Remember what I said last night? I only want you, Daniel. No one else."

He nodded and kissed my forehead. "Yes, I remember. And I know that up here," he said, pointing to his head. "But that guy has the hots for you, Trudie, and that really gets to me. I can't help it."

"I know." I thought about Sherrie Flowers and the way her

deliberate moves on Daniel affected me. "Do you think you can lighten up a little so we can all enjoy the rest of Mom's Thanksgiving dinner? It means so much to her."

"I guess I owe her an apology," he said, kissing the top of my head. "And you. I'm sorry, Trudie. I've been behaving like a spoiled child. Let's get back in there."

As we re-entered the dining room, Daniel glanced at Alan but didn't say anything.

Alan nodded to him then put his napkin on the table. "Thank you, Mrs. Fine, for including me in this wonderful dinner, but I have an early court date in the morning and some homework to do tonight."

"But you can't leave so early," Mom said. "We still have dessert coming."

Alan stood and glanced at me. "No, I really do need to leave. But thank you."

"Then let me pack some leftovers for you."

"No, really Helen. I do have to go."

"I'll get the door for you," I said, starting to get up. Daniel put his hand on my arm and looked up at me with a frown.

I raised my eyebrows at him and he took his hand away.

Alan smiled. "Don't get up, Trudie. I can let myself out."

After the front door closed, the silence and Alan's empty chair dominated the room.

Mom got up and began to clear his place. "I'm sorry." She shook her head. "I guess I made a mistake inviting Mr. Bernstein. I just thought he needed a place to go for the holidays. Everyone should have a place to go on Thanksgiving." Her voice was thick and sounded close to tears.

"No, Helen. I'm sorry," Daniel said, rising to help clear away Alan's dirty dishes. "It was all my fault."

"Don't be silly. It's all right." Mom brightened. "As a matter of fact, this is the day to be thankful and, as is our tradition at this table, let's find out what each of us is thankful for." This part of the meal, I knew, had always been her favorite. As she sat back down, her mood had transformed, her joy palpable, and I wouldn't have been surprised if my mother began clapping with glee. "I'll go first," she said. "I am thankful to have all of you, family and friends, to share our home and our table today."

She turned to Daniel.

"I'm thankful you haven't kicked me out of this house for my rudeness," he said.

We laughed.

"No, really Daniel," I said.

He looked me in the eye and put his hand on my cheek. "I'm thankful to have you in my life."

"And I'm thankful to have you in my life," I said to him.

We all turned to Dad. "I am thankful to be able to enjoy this outstanding meal." He rubbed his belly in a circular motion.

Katie looked around shyly and in her quiet voice said, "Thank you for including me in your tradition. I'm thankful for your good food, warmth, and friendship. And for offering your babysitting services," she added, looking at Mom.

Everyone laughed.

Will cleared his throat. "I am thankful for the best Thanksgiving I've had in quite some time—and for new friends." He turned to Katie.

"Well, now that you've all indulged me," Mom said, heading into the kitchen, "Dessert will be served in the family room."

As Katie began to get up, she lost her balance and grabbed for the table, overturning the gravy boat.

Will caught Katie's arm to keep her from falling, a quick, reflexive movement, but too late to avoid the brown, clotted liquid oozing over the edge of the table and onto his lap.

Looking down at the disaster, Katie's eyes widened. "Will, your shoes."

I froze, thinking about those pure white cross trainers he'd strode in on and wondering how he'd react.

But he looked up into Katie's face and said, "Are you all right?"

"Uh-huh," she nodded. "You?"

They both peered down at his lap and Katie grabbed her napkin and began to dab at Will's pants, then reddened and began to giggle. Will chuckled along with her as together they attempted to clean up the mess while my mother ran to the kitchen for some paper towels.

I walked around to their side of the table to assess the damage, biting my bottom lip to keep from snickering. The stains weren't as evident on Will's dark wash jeans, but his shoes, white with swirls of brown gravy, resembled two loaves of marble pound cake.

Once everyone was settled in the family room, Mom and I brought in the pumpkin and apple pies and steaming mugs of hot chocolate, while Dad went to the kitchen and returned with the makings for S'mores. We took turns toasting marshmallows over the burning logs and licking our sticky fingers.

When it was time to leave, Daniel asked, "Ready to go, Katie?"

Will turned to her. "If it's okay with you, I'd like to drive you home."

"Sure," she said, coloring a little. Then she hugged my father and mother and thanked them for a lovely evening.

Daniel and I got into his car, and he leaned over to kiss me. "This is exactly what I want for us every Thanksgiving. Family, friends, an abundance of food…"

"…and football," I said, continuing his alliterative list.

He laughed then his face became more serious. "No, really. This is what I want for us—always."

"Me, too."

Silent, we gazed at each other for a moment. I waited, willing him to continue. Say it, I thought. Say it.

The expression on Daniel's face told me he wanted to say more. Then he turned away, started the engine, and backed out of the driveway.

Chapter Fifteen

My car sped down I-270, faster and faster. I tried the brake pedal, but it felt like a plastic toy with its spring broken. I kept stomping on the pedal, but the car would not stop. The needle on the speedometer moved higher and higher.

Even worse, I couldn't see out the windshield. Every window was tinted black. When I tried to see out of the car, I could only see my own reflection. I knew any moment my car would crash, tumble, and burn.

I heard a knock, knock, knock. Someone rapped on the window trying to talk to me. "Trudie, are you in there?"

They were pulling on the door handle, trying to jiggle the key in the lock.

Then a bell. A doorbell.

I opened my eyes and realized I was in bed. Just a dream. I exhaled my relief.

Knock, knock, knock.

Someone really was at the door. I checked the clock. It was only eight. I'd set my alarm for eight-thirty. Who would be at the door so early?

Daniel's side of the bed was empty, and I remembered he'd had to work today.

His flannel shirt that I'd worn to bed came almost to my knees. But I grabbed my robe and went to the door. "Who is it?"

"Trudie, it's Rose. And Zeus."

"Rose," I said, pulling the door open. She stood on the porch wearing a puffy white ski jacket and black fur-lined boots.

"Can we come in? It's pretty chilly out here."

"Sure." I stood back to let them enter and Zeus looked up at Rose with a whine until she signaled it was okay for him to greet me. I knelt to scratch his head and gave him a kiss.

"I hope I didn't wake you, Trudie. But by the looks of you, I think I did."

Do I look that bad? I thought. I finger-combed my hair to smooth it back. "It's okay. I was getting up soon anyway. Zach and I have work to do for an event tomorrow night. And, to be honest, I'm glad you woke me. I was having an awful dream. But come into the kitchen and we'll have some coffee."

Pulling off her parka, Rose hung it on the coat tree and followed me down the hall. She wore an oversized gray sweatshirt and black leggings. "What was your dream about?"

I shuddered. "Just a combination of all the craziness in my life lately. Here, sit." I pointed to a kitchen chair and went to the sink to fill the coffee pot with water.

Rose laughed. "Good dog." I turned to see Zeus sitting obediently.

"I guess he thought I was talking to him, huh? How come you're out so early?" I asked.

"Well, I'd planned to tell you I was out shopping for deals on art supplies. You know, today is Black Friday."

"Oh, yeah. I should check the ads to see what they're giving away." I poured the water into the coffee maker, put in a filter, and counted out four scoops of coffee before flipping the switch. "So the real reason you're here?"

"I want you to take Zeus for a while," she said. "And I knew if I called first, you'd say no."

"Take Zeus? Why? He's your pride and joy." I took the foil off a paper plate with the leftover slices of pie my mother had sent home with me. As if I needed to eat more pie.

"I don't mean you should take him permanently. Just for a while. You've had too many disturbing things happen lately. Jennifer told me about the incident with the clown doll the other night. I think you need protection until they find Christine's killer."

"How did Jennifer know about that?"

"Zach told her. Uh-oh. I hope I'm not getting him into trouble for that. But really, Trudie. I think you'll feel safer having Zeus by your side."

I brought the pie over to the table along with plates, napkins and forks. "Like a guard dog, you mean?"

"Exactly." Rose put a slice of pumpkin pie on her plate and looked up. "Got any whipped cream?"

"Not sure. Let me check." I located a can and checked the sell-by date. "I think this is still okay to use."

Rose held the can upside down and coaxed out a pretty white rosette onto her pie then licked her finger and looked up at me. "Trudie, Jennifer and I are really worried about you. Zach is, too. You can take Zeus with you everywhere you go. He has great instincts about people. He'll know before you do if someone is lurking in the shadows."

"I appreciate what you're trying to do, Rose. But I can't take Zeus. He's your dog. He should be with you. He loves to watch you work. He doesn't make a move without you."

"Who just told him to sit, and he obeyed? He loves you, too. Trudie, I think you'd feel more comfortable having him around to protect you. Look, it would just be for a week or two. Maybe more."

I thought about my coming home the other night and my fear that someone was waiting for me on the lawn outside or that an intruder might still be in the house. Zeus would have known what was rustling the leaves outside. And he would have known if someone was hiding inside. But taking care of a dog was a big responsibility, feeding him, taking him out for walks, being home more often. "I couldn't bring a dog to my catering jobs," I said.

"Then you'll drop him off at our house." She smiled. "We'll dog sit for you."

A beep from the coffee maker signaled that the brew was ready. I poured coffee into two mugs and put out the milk and sugar. My first cup of the day usually cleared my head and helped me focus. I took a sip, comforted by the way it warmed me all the way through.

Zeus sniffed at my robe and flannel shirt. I'm sure Daniel's scent lingered after a night in bed with him. Daniel. How would he feel about having a dog living in his house?

He'd probably agree that I could use a dog's protection.

"What about all his stuff?" I asked. "His dog bed, his halter, his bowls, food, Jennifer's biscuits. Zeus comes with a lot of accessories."

"Not that much. It's all in the car." Rose eyed me as she sipped her coffee.

"In the car? You were pretty sure I'd agree to this, weren't you?" She grinned. "Yep, I guess I was."

I bent down to Zeus so we were nose to nose. "I guess you'll be living here for a while, buddy."

AS I ENTERED the office, Zach's eyes widened when he noticed Zeus by my side. He stood and approached from behind the desk. "Hey, Zeus. What are you doing here?" He knelt and ruffled the dog's hair and then glanced up at me.

"He's my companion for a while. Rose thought I needed a protector."

Zach got up and looked me in the eye. "I agree with that one hundred percent. You need someone with you day and night. I'm worried about you."

"Zach, you are always worried about me. Everyone worries about me. I'm fine. After all, I live with a cop."

"Yeah, but the cop isn't always there. And I can hardly count all the times you've been in jeopardy just in the past six months." He put his hands on my shoulders. "Promise me you'll be careful, Trudie. You're my partner—and my best friend. I love you and I don't want to lose you."

I gazed back at Zach. "I love you, too," I said quietly.

"Then promise me."

"Okay, I promise."

"Promise what?" His gaze was challenging.

I twisted from his grasp and pulled my copy of Julia Child's *Joy of Cooking* off the book shelf on the wall. Then, placing my left hand on my culinary bible, I held up my right hand. "I promise I'll be careful."

"And you'll stay away from anyone or any place that could pose a danger to you."

"Zach, this is silly."

"Say it, Trudie."

"Okay, okay. I'll stay away from anyone or any place that could pose a danger to me. Are you satisfied now?" I asked, replacing the book and sitting down at the desk. Zeus followed and sat beside my chair like the guard dog he was.

"I guess." Zach shook his head. "Now let's get to work."

The next night, we would be catering a charity benefit to raise research funds for a rare type of cancer. About one hundred people were expected for dinner and dancing at a new local venue.

"I've been making a list of ingredients we have to pick up for tomorrow night." Zach pointed to the computer screen. "Check out the spreadsheet and see if I've missed anything."

I moved the mouse back and forth to wake up the monitor. The chart Zach had created showed each dish we would be preparing, the ingredients needed, and where and when we would pick them up and do the prep work. He'd also divided up the tasks between us.

"This is great, Zach. It will really keep us organized. Where did you come up with an idea like this?"

"From Ally's software program at her restaurant. Of course, we can't afford anything like that yet, but I can mimic some of the features. And see." He leaned over Zeus to grab the mouse.

"We can color the cells as each task is done. We can even download it to our phones."

"Love it. I'm excited to try it out for tomorrow's gig. And speaking of Ally, how was Thanksgiving at her restaurant?"

Zach straightened. "Couldn't have been better. She had a full house, but the staff really held their own, got the dishes out on a timely basis. The customers were raving about the food."

"I'm glad. Do you think she can…?" I hesitated. "I mean, her first restaurant had a great opening, too, and was really successful the first year. But then she…"

"I know what you're thinking." Zach's expression became stony. "Ally got bored with her first restaurant, hired the wrong person to oversee it, and he drove it out of business. But she's changed since then. The idea of a restaurant serving healthy comfort food was all hers, and she's been involved with planning every aspect of the project from beginning to end. She's more excited about *Savor* than I've ever seen her before, and once she's had a little time under her belt, she plans to expand into a local chain."

Zach's eyes became bright with emotion as he spoke, and I realized I'd put him in the position of defending Ally. I'd been worried about his involvement and investment of time, and whether Ally could sustain her enthusiasm this time around.

"I'm sorry," I said. "I shouldn't have even brought it up. I can see that she's changed and know this is only the start of something big. And Zach, she sure is lucky to have you onboard as her friend and advocate."

He smiled. "Thanks."

After about an hour of going over details for the event, Zeus whined, bringing me back to reality.

"Time for a walk, huh?" I said, putting on my coat and grabbing his leash.

Zeus perked his ears up and wagged his tail.

"Well, this dog-watching isn't too bad," I said to Zach. "He lets me know what he wants and I comply."

Zach smirked. "Yeah, so who's training who?"

"Does it matter? We're getting along fine." Hooking the leash to his halter, I started for the door.

"Forget something?" Zach asked, pulling a couple of plastic bags out of the duffel Rose had packed for Zeus.

"Oh, yeah," I said, taking them from Zach and feeling a little dubious about how easy this dog-walking was going to be.

I led Zeus out the front door into the parking lot to find some type of grassy area. Nothing on our part of Nebel Street with all its industrial warehouses and parking lots. But I noticed a grassy area across the street and about a block down the hill by a condo development. We headed that way.

Checking in both directions, I crossed the street, Zeus trotting along next to me. A jogger, wearing a gray hooded sweatshirt, was approaching down the sidewalk toward us, so I moved aside to let him pass. With his hood up and obscuring his hair and face, I couldn't tell if he was male or female, teen or adult. The runner didn't slow at all on the narrow walkway and, as he blew past us, he shoved me to the ground.

I landed on my stomach, emitting an *oomph* sound as the air knocked out of me. Trying to catch my breath, I pushed myself up and sat back on the concrete sidewalk.

Zeus snarled and tried to run after the jogger, but with his leash still held firmly in my hand, almost dragged me with him. He whined, straining against the leash and looking back and forth between me and the jogger, who had now disappeared around a curve.

"It's okay, Zeus. I'm all right." I held out my hands and he wagged himself into my arms, licking my face. Both of my pants legs had holes in the knees, which I could see were skinned and bleeding.

I noticed a folded piece of paper lying on the ground next to me and felt the hairs on my neck stand at attention. I picked it up and opened it, knowing exactly what it would say.

"You told."

Struggling to my feet, I found a small strip of grass for Zeus to do his business and pulled out my cellphone to call Daniel.

Chapter Sixteen

Nebel Street buzzed with police activity. It must have been a slow day for the county police because cruisers were parked on both sides, lights flashing and radios blaring communications back and forth to headquarters.

Daniel held me close as we stood outside *A Fine Fix* watching the investigators, Zeus sitting obediently beside us.

"Thank god Zeus was with you." Daniel said. "Who knows what that guy would have done if you'd been alone."

"But I wouldn't have even been outside if I didn't have to walk Zeus. I would have been safely inside the office working with Zach. So what does that tell you?"

Daniel brushed the windblown hair out of my face and frowned. "It tells me that someone is out to get you, and it's a good thing you had Zeus to protect you. Whether you were walking the dog or walking to your car, they were ready for you. Someone knew you had the dog with you and that you'd eventually be taking him out for a walk. Who besides Rose would have known that? Somehow, it always seems to point in her direction, doesn't it?"

I took a step back from Daniel and shook my head. "No. I won't believe Rose is responsible. Whoever is doing these things wants us to believe it's Rose. Maybe they've been watching me and knew I had Zeus with me. That's plausible, isn't it?"

Daniel pulled me close again and kissed the top of my head. "Yes, it is. But I've got my eye on everyone. In the meantime, I'll post an officer here and at the house to keep an eye on things. And you keep Zeus with you whenever possible, okay?"

"Okay. I can't bring a dog to the job tomorrow night, but he'll be with me until then. Speaking of that job, Zach and I have lots of shopping and prep work to do, so I'll see you later."

ZACH HAD LEFT the office to pick up the liquor and non-perishables. In the morning, we expected an early delivery of fresh rockfish, tenderloin and produce.

I spent the next hour making calls to confirm the final number of attendees, the room setup, deliveries of the rented table linens and centerpieces, and the number of bartenders and servers who'd be working the event, with a special request for Gordon to help serve. Then I called Jennifer to make arrangements to pick up the fresh rolls and breads and the dessert tarts.

"Trudie, I was just going to call you," Jennifer said. "I contacted Amy at the gallery, and she has the tally of Rose's art pieces sold. I told her I want to come by to see what's left and pick up the check for

Rose."

"Why do you want to do that when she can just mail it to you?"

"With all of the police activity and cleanup going on over there, Rose asked me to inspect the unsold pieces to make sure they haven't been damaged before they're returned to her. The thing is, I'm leery about going to the gallery by myself, and you had offered to come along. Would you still do that?"

I swallowed the lump in my throat. The thought of returning to the gallery where a gruesome murder had been committed and where I'd almost lost my own life when my brakes were cut was inconceivable. Plus, I had promised Daniel and Zach that I would stay away from any place that might pose a danger.

"I don't know, Jennifer. I'm really busy today and tomorrow getting ready for our event tomorrow night. And truthfully, I'm just as spooked as you are about going back to the gallery."

"I know. I wouldn't even ask you except I really want to do this for Rose since the court order says she's not allowed to get anywhere near the gallery. If I can get that money for her and her unsold pieces back, it would make her so happy. And god knows she needs something to brighten her life. What about Sunday afternoon? Your event will be over and so will the morning rush at the coffee shop. We can even bring Zeus with us for protection."

As I held the phone receiver, my hand felt cold and sweaty. Listening to Jennifer's reasoning, it all sounded harmless, the two of us going to the gallery with Zeus, picking up Rose's payment and checking out the unsold artwork. But Daniel would never agree to my going back to the gallery. On the other hand, I had been the one to suggest this to Jennifer in the first place.

"Give me time to think about it," I said. "Maybe by Sunday there will be a break in the case."

"Fair enough," Jennifer said. "In the meantime, I'll have your baked goods boxed and ready by ten tomorrow morning."

I breathed my relief. For now, I didn't have to worry about making a trip to the gallery. The decision might be easier on Sunday morning. Time would tell.

ZACH AND I began our prep work early on Saturday morning. I'd set up Zeus's bed in a spot away from the food, where he obediently remained. Any necessary walks that day were made in the parking lot right outside the office with the police officer on watch close at hand.

While I prepared the hors d'oeuvres—bruschetta, tuna tartare, mushrooms stuffed with crabmeat, and chicken satay—Zach painstakingly built the vegetable Napoleons, layers of roasted zucchini, yellow squash, eggplant, and red peppers, which would be served with the rockfish and a puree of purple potatoes.

This was the part of catering we enjoyed most, Zach and me working side by side as we'd done since childhood.

"No one can layer those vegetables so artistically as you," I said, admiring Zach's work.

"Decorating wedding cakes with Jennifer has been great training for this. Every detail has to be perfect when you're adding rosettes or lace or patterns."

"Jennifer's working out to be a great partner for us, isn't she?" I said.

Zach evened out the small stack of veggies in front of him and moved it into one of the foil pans we'd be using to transfer the food. "Yep. I think she's helped put our business on another level. So many of our clients come from referrals now. We're lucky to have her onboard."

I swirled the tuna tartare onto each in a row of cucumber slices. "She's never said no to us once, has she? Even when we've had last minute jobs."

Zach stood and looked at me. "No, she's never declined our requests. What brought this on?"

I hesitated. "So if Jennifer asked us for a favor, whatever it was, we probably wouldn't refuse her, would we?"

"Probably not. I guess it would depend what she wanted. Why do you ask?" He continued his own assembly line, making rows of the first layer, then the next and the next until he'd completed the stacks, evened them out and packed them with the others.

I shrugged. "I don't know. Just thinking, that's all."

Next, we worked on the starters. Zach used the blender to puree the butternut squash with Granny Smith apples and spices to create a creamy soup while I diced the Asian pears and candied walnuts for the salad.

It was important to prep, pack, and refrigerate all these items first so we could begin deboning the rockfish filets. I cleaned the work surfaces while Zach wheeled over a cart of fifty filets of fish immersed in ice. Together, removing each v-shaped wedge of bones with our knives, we had the job done in about a half hour. Slicing the seventy servings of tenderloin took a lot less time and effort.

With the prepping completed, Zach drove us in the van to Jennifer's coffee shop to pick up our baked goods. We had to leave Zeus in the warehouse. This was the part of dog ownership that bothered me, but we'd only be gone about an hour.

When we pulled up in front of the coffee shop, I spotted Will leaving May's restaurant, *Maybelline's*, located on the same block. Oh no, I thought. Was something wrong? Why would they need a police visit. Had May been robbed?

"You go ahead, Zach. Jennifer has everything boxed up for us. I'm just going to pop into *Maybelline's* for a minute."

"I don't know, Trudie. The last time I left you on your own there, you were trapped in a restaurant fire."

"Zach, that was months ago. What are the odds it would happen again? Plus my visit is totally unexpected."

"Well, all right. But as soon as I have the boxes in the van, I'm coming to get you."

I headed the half block to the restaurant and opened the front door. It was lunch time on a Saturday, and several tables were occupied. Gina, who was waiting on a corner table, gave me a quick wave. Everything seemed normal.

Katie emerged from the kitchen, spotted me and came to greet me. "Trudie, are you here for lunch?"

"No. Is everything okay here? I noticed Will leaving the restaurant and thought there might be a problem."

Katie reddened. "No. Everything's fine. Will just…well, he came by to say hello and to ask me out."

I realized my mouth was open and then broke into a big grin. "He asked you out? I knew the two of you were getting along well at Thanksgiving, but I didn't realize…I mean, wow. He asked you out. And you said?"

Katie peered down at her feet and put her hand on her belly. Her neck and ears had turned pink. "I said yes, of course. Will's a nice guy. A little too buttoned up maybe. But I think I can loosen him up."

"That's great," I said. "He can use some loosening up. I'm glad you two hit it off."

"Just friends for now," she said. "And Trudie, thanks so much for inviting me to your mom's for Thanksgiving dinner. I sent her a note. I really enjoyed the whole family atmosphere. You're lucky you grew up with that."

"Yes, I'm very lucky. And glad you were able to come." I smiled at Katie again. "You and Will, huh? Wow."

I headed back to the coffee shop and found Zach in the kitchen with Jennifer ready to take the last couple of boxes to the van.

"See, Zach." I said. "I'm here. No problems. Hi, Jennifer."

"No problems with what?" she asked.

"Just Zach in his worry mode again. Are you ready to go?" I asked him. "I hate leaving Zeus by himself for too long."

Jennifer laughed. "Spoken like a new pet owner. Zeus will be fine.

He's used to being left alone during the day. By the way," she said, her tone more serious. "Have you thought about what I asked the other day?"

I glanced at Zach, who raised his eyebrows in a question. I didn't want him to know anything about what Jennifer had asked me to do. He, like Daniel, would never agree to my going to the gallery.

"I-I've been pretty busy today, Jennifer. I'll speak to you in the morning."

She looked back and forth between me and Zach, and hopefully realized my reluctance to talk about it in front of him. "Okay. Tomorrow then."

"What?" Zach asked.

Jennifer waved her hand through the air. "Just girl stuff. Nothing you need to know."

The venue for the charity benefit that night was a new meeting space on the top floor of a building with high ceilings and wall-to-wall windows that overlooked the glittering lights of a busy retail and residential area.

Our servers and bartenders dressed in all black with purple bowties, and I wore my black apron with *A Fine Fix* scrolled in purple script. I greeted Gordon warmly, but resisted the impulse to give him a motherly hug. He seemed to understand our system and, once Zach had filled him in on the details of the event, Gordon took the lead with the rest of the staff, making me feel like a proud mama.

The passed hors d'oeuvres during cocktail hour were a big hit, the room set with high-tops, white sofas and easy chairs placed in small conversational groupings.

For added interest, the set-up in the dining area was a mix of round, square and rectangular tables, with high and low floral centerpieces. The tablecloth overlays were a shimmering, translucent silver fabric covering traditional white linens.

We'd been informed ahead of time that the guests, who were dressed in cocktail attire, were important donors to the foundation and needed to be served with the utmost care. This was not a problem for us. Whether catering for wealthy philanthropists or seniors for Thanksgiving dinner at a community center, all were treated with equal respect and outstanding food and service. We knew that each successful function led to many more.

The eight-piece band was headlined by a female singer. Their repertoire began with a big-band sound to start during dinner. Afterward, a heart-wrenching video showed the devastating effects of the disease, followed by a cancer specialist and a researcher who told of the advances being made toward a cure, but of course, funding was desperately needed.

During dessert, the band struck a livelier chord playing more contemporary music that tempted guests onto the dance floor. Of course, the open bar may have had something to do with that as well.

Zach and I stood on the sidelines, enjoying the perfection of this successful event, with no issues, no complaints and, thankfully, no murders

Chapter Seventeen

Zach drove me home in the van and watched until I let myself into the house. With Daniel at home, the security officer who'd been posted outside the house all day had left. Tonight, lights blazed in every room, and Daniel dozed in front of the TV, which he had tuned in to the Food Network, a channel he would never have chosen for himself. Zeus, curled up on the sofa next to Daniel, opened one eye and greeted me with a slight swish of his tail. So much for my two protectors.

I took off my shoes and cuddled into Daniel's other side. On the TV, I recognized an episode of *Chopped* that I'd already seen, where contestants had to use leftover Thanksgiving foods to create delicious, well-plated appetizers, entrees, and desserts. I often fantasized about being on the show. Sitting at home watching, I usually could come up with the dishes I would create. But I was sure that if I were a contestant opening each box of surprise ingredients, I would freeze up like a TV dinner.

Daniel opened his eyes and smiled at me.

I leaned toward him and kissed him on the lips. "Thank you."

"For what?" He raised his eyebrows at me.

"For welcoming me home with all the lights on and the TV tuned into my favorite channel. For being here waiting for me."

"I fell asleep."

"Yes, but you're here for me. That means a lot." I kissed him again. Zeus put his head on Daniel's chest to get closer, so I kissed him, too.

"Thanks, guys." I yawned. It was one a.m. "Let's go to bed."

As Daniel and I got up from the sofa, Zeus scrambled to the front door, dancing and panting at us.

"Really, Zeus? You want to go out at this hour?" I said.

Daniel stretched and reached for his shoes. "I'll take him out. You get ready for bed, Trudie. I'll be in soon."

"Okay. Sorry. This dog-watching thing has some disadvantages, doesn't it?

"A few. But I'm glad he's here to take care of you."

In the foyer, Daniel took his parka from the coat tree and put it on. Then he hooked the leash on Zeus's halter and the two of them headed out for their walk.

I plodded into the bedroom to change my clothes and then into the bathroom to wash up. Getting into bed, I checked the time on my phone. They'd been gone for ten minutes. I thought this was going to be a short walk.

I heard the front door close. "Daniel?"

No answer.

"Daniel? Zeus?" No response.

Hadn't they heard me? I wanted to check to see where they were, but something told me to stay put. I wondered if Daniel had taken his phone with him. When I tried his number, I heard it ringing from the living room. My stomach skittered like popcorn kernels in a microwave.

Finally, the front door opened and I heard Zeus scrabbling across the hardwood floor.

"Daniel," I called.

"Trudie." I heard Daniel's footsteps as he approached and flung the bedroom door open. "Are you okay?" he asked.

"I'm fine. What's wrong?"

He took my hand and led me to the foyer. A clown doll hung from the light fixture, the same horror-stricken porcelain head lolling to the side and another note pinned to its body.

I gasped. "Oh my god. Just a few minutes ago, I heard the front door close but I thought it was you. Who is doing this and how are they getting in the house?"

"I'm not sure," Daniel said. "I locked the door when I left."

We both peered down at Zeus, who was sniffing around the floor and the front door.

"Come with me, Zeus." Daniel led him from room to room, but eventually Zeus returned to the foyer where he continued to sniff at the door.

Daniel retrieved two plastic bags and put on a pair of latex gloves. He unpinned the note and unfolded it twice. "You told," it read. He put the note in one bag and the clown doll in the other then called the station.

"No," he said into the phone. "Don't bother coming tonight. I've got the evidence bagged, and I have reason to believe the intruder didn't go beyond the front hall. But somehow, this person had access to the house. I'm setting the alarm now and tomorrow I'll have the locks changed."

I'd begun to shiver, and Daniel walked me into the bedroom, and lay down beside me, tucking the blanket securely around my body.

"I'm scared, Daniel. They must have come in when I was in the bathroom. I was alone in this house with the intruder."

"It's okay, Trudie. I won't let this happen ever again."

He pulled my body against his and held me while I cried myself to sleep.

SUNLIGHT BATHED THE room, and I woke to Zeus's kisses.

"Good morning, sleepy." Daniel stood at the foot of the bed with a breakfast tray.

I stretched and yawned. "Good morning." Then it all came back to me, the clown, the note, the intruder. I sat up and leaned against the headboard. It was hard to believe someone could have slipped into the house so effortlessly in the few moments Daniel had been out. "I could use that coffee."

"It's our day off," he said. "Let's just hang out today. We'll read the paper, watch some old movies, take a walk."

"Sounds heavenly to me." In the back of my mind, I thought there was something I was going to do today. Whatever it was, it must not have been important. The only thing I wanted was a day of normalcy with my guy.

I took a bite of my English muffin, enjoying the crunch and the melted butter permeating all the nooks and crannies. Daniel sat next to me in bed, savoring his own cup of coffee as he leafed through the Sports page of the *Post* while I checked out the latest restaurant review in the Sunday magazine.

"This is nice," I said. "We should do this every Sunday."

"When I don't have to work and you don't have a catering job. How often do we get a day off together like this?"

"Not very often," I agreed.

The phone rang.

"Oh, no," I said. "Don't answer it. Please. Someone wants one of us to do something."

Daniel laughed and shrugged and picked up the phone. "It's for you," he said holding out the receiver to me.

"Who?"

"It's Jennifer."

"Oh," I said, remembering. Then I thought, oh no. The gallery. I felt as if a dozen eggs had just slipped out of my hands, all of them cracking open on the floor.

Daniel eyed me as I took the phone.

"Hi, Jennifer."

"Hope it's not too early to call. You know me. I'm here at five-thirty every morning baking up a storm. Have you decided about going with me to the gallery this afternoon?"

I glanced at Daniel and thought about the second clown doll hanging in the foyer last night and the intruder. I shivered. "I'm not going to be able to go with you. I just can't."

"Can't or won't? Trudie, I really need you to come with me. I've got to do this for Rose and I don't have anyone else to ask."

I closed my eyes. Now she was going to try to guilt me into going with her. I hated turning down friends' requests. That was probably why people were always asking me to help them with things. "My plans have changed, and I won't be able to do it."

"All right. Not today. What about tomorrow?" Apparently, she was going to persist until I gave in to her.

"I don't know. Maybe." I turned away from Daniel, who hadn't taken his eyes off me for the entire call. "I'll have to let you know. I'm sorry, Jennifer. Today just is not a good day. I'll speak to you tomorrow."

"What does Jennifer want you to do?" he asked after I'd hung up the phone. "I can see it has you freaked."

For a moment, I considered asking Daniel to go with us to the gallery that afternoon, but the thought of spending a whole day with him, just the two of us on a gorgeous autumn day, was such a rare opportunity and something I just wasn't willing to give up.

"She wants me to…"

Daniel's cellphone rang. "Yeah. Goldman here," he said into the phone. He stood and began pacing the room. "Now? You've got to be kidding." He looked at me. "No, this is not a good time. Okay, okay.

I'll be there in twenty minutes."

"Sorry, Trudie," he said. "It's one of those things. I have to go. I'm sorry to spoil our Sunday together." He was already in the closet pulling out his pants and shirt.

"What about reading the paper and watching old movies and taking a walk?"

He came over to me in bed and bent to kiss me. "I'm sorry. I'll make it up to you next Sunday. Really, I won't let anything get in our way."

"But next Sunday, Zach and I have a brunch to cater. Can't you get someone else to fill in for you today?"

"No. It's my case. Sorry, honey. With any luck, I'll be home sometime this afternoon."

"With any luck," I spouted back at him, "I may be home this afternoon. Maybe not."

He stopped and turned to me. "Hey, didn't Jennifer want you to do something with her? Why don't you go, you two girls? Maybe you can take Zeus with you."

I opened my mouth to speak, to tell him what he was actually suggesting. But my anger and disappointment got the better of me. "Maybe I will."

When Daniel left the house, I picked up the phone. "Jennifer, I've changed my mind. What time do you want me to pick you up?"

Chapter Eighteen

With Zeus in the car, I picked up Jennifer at two-thirty. It was one of those perfect fall days with a cloudless azure sky and the air more crisp and clear than an uncooked cellophane noodle. It was a day meant for lovers to walk hand-in-hand through the crackling leaves. But that wasn't going to happen for me today. By now, I should have been more understanding of Daniel and the demands of his job. But imagining the way this day could have gone, it was hard not to feel some resentment.

Jennifer waved as she emerged from the coffee shop holding a paper bag.

"What's that?" The scent of something fresh-baked and delectable filled the car.

"Chocolate croissants," she said. "It never hurts to come bearing gifts."

"Good thinking."

Zeus stuck his head between the seats and licked Jennifer's ear.

"Hey, boy. We miss you at home." She ruffled the top of his head and pulled a dog biscuit from her pocket. "No, I didn't forget you."

The downtown traffic wasn't too bad on the last day of Thanksgiving weekend, and we made it across town to Dupont Circle in about fifteen minutes. At the bottom of the driveway, I hesitated, wondering if I should look for street parking rather than risking another car-tampering episode. But the thought of climbing the gallery's steep driveway and arriving at the front door perspiring and out-of-breath caused me to turn in and let my car take the hill.

I parked next to a black SUV and a silver Acura. I assumed these belonged to Rick and Amy since the gallery hadn't reopened yet. Our knocking on the back door didn't produce any response, so we took the flagstone path around to the front door and used the doorbell. I heard footsteps approaching and recalled the polished hardwood floor inside the gallery which also stirred up a disturbing vision of broken glass and spilled wine from that fateful night. What the hamburger was I doing back here?

It took me a moment to recognize Amy when she opened the door. The only way to describe her was sleek, her hair pulled back into a bun, her red lips full and eyes perfectly lined with black pencil. Her body was squeezed into a black sleeveless sheath dress that ended above her knees. Even though she was a couple of inches taller than me, with the leopard print stiletto heels she wore today, I had to crane my neck to look up at her. Could this be the same frumpy Amy I'd first met with the boxy dress and clunky pumps?

"Hello, Jennifer. And Trudie, what a surprise." She stepped back, opened the door wider and Zeus nosed himself inside. "What's he doing here? No dogs allowed in the gallery. He'll scratch up the floors."

"It's okay," Jennifer said. "Rose keeps his nails clipped. We never have a problem with him scratching the floors at home."

Amy shook her head. "I don't know. Too many things for him to get into." She held her hand out toward the dog in a half-hearted effort to pet him.

Zeus backed away and emitted a low rumble that resonated through the hallway. The hair along his back stood ridged in alert, confirming my own dubious feelings about her.

Amy pulled her hand away and straightened. "I don't know about this."

"Look, I've got him on a leash," Jennifer said. "He's not going anywhere. Can we just come in a get our business taken care of? Then we'll be out of here."

"Well, I guess it's all right."

Following Amy to her office, our footsteps echoed in the gallery, which appeared smaller without any art work on display. I wondered what they'd done with Rose's paintings and sculptures that had graced the walls and filled the rooms the night of the opening.

As if reading my mind, Amy said over her shoulder, "We're getting ready for our next showing Thursday night. Moving in works from another artist tomorrow."

"Where are Rose's pieces?" Jennifer asked. "The ones that didn't sell."

"In the storage area," Amy said as we entered her office. Not only had all the fingerprint dust been cleaned away, but it looked like an entirely different office, far grander than before. It had the obvious touches of a professional decorator with its oversized ivory desk that looked antique, matching high-back chairs and even a French blue upholstered sofa and chair adorned with patterned pillows that coordinated with the drapes. The room felt more like a Paris salon than an office.

"Wasn't this Christine's office?" Jennifer asked. "Seems like it would feel a little creepy working in here where—you know."

Amy stood erect behind the desk. "Where my aunt was murdered? Actually, it gives me more of a sense of her, and it comforts me."

"Hello, ladies."

We all turned to the doorway where Rick stood. Tanned and looking more attractive than ever in his tailored trousers and fitted pullover sweater, he gave us a smile that shot through me like a habanero pepper. He strolled into the office and stooped, holding out his hand for Zeus to smell. The dog wagged his tail and investigated his scent. Rick looked up at us. "I guess you're here to pick up Rose's commission."

"Yes," Jennifer said. "And to check out the unsold pieces."

"What have you got there?" Rick asked, sniffing the air and nodding toward the bag in her hand.

"Oh, I almost forgot." Jennifer held the bag out to Amy. "I brought you some pastries I baked this morning."

Amy wrinkled her nose as she took the bag and, as if it were a satchel of garbage, held it in the tips of her fingers, exposing long, red fingernails. She stretched out her arm to Rick. "Here. Take this into the kitchen, would you?"

Rick opened the bag and peered inside then pulled out a croissant and took a bite, flakes of pastry taking refuge on his sweater. He nodded approvingly, brushing the crumbs to the floor. "Excellent. Nice to see you ladies." He smiled and took another bite of the croissant as he left the room.

"Let's get down to business. Sit, please." Amy pointed to the pair of chairs in front of her desk and lowered herself into her own chair which, with its scrolling ivory arms and trim, resembled a throne. She opened a drawer, extracted a white business envelope, and handed it to Jennifer. "This is a detailed listing of each piece sold, the selling price, and Rose's commission. A check is included."

Jennifer opened the envelope, pulled out a sheet of paper and unfolded it to read. "Wait a minute. This is all that sold? Only four pieces?"

"You need to remember that the evening was interrupted in a chaotic way. There were some guests who showed interest in buying, but after what happened to Aunt Christine, those we contacted over the days following didn't want to have anything to do with Rose's artwork, especially after she'd been arrested for the murder."

Jennifer dipped her head to the list again. "I see."

"Consequently," Amy continued, "our storage area is overflowing with the unsold works. Those sculptures are monstrous. They need to be removed by Wednesday to make room for the next show."

"I don't know if I can arrange that by Wednesday," Jennifer said.

"I can contact a service we use. But Rose will be responsible for the cost of the move."

Amy sat straighter in her chair. "As noted in her contract, the gallery incurred the cost of moving the artwork here. But we are not responsible for return of unsold works."

Jennifer pulled the commission check out of the envelope. "Wait. You've only paid Rose fifty percent. She expected sixty. This will barely cover the price of transporting her work."

"Read the contract that Rose signed. The gallery gets fifty. She gets the same."

I remembered overhearing Rose and Christine's argument about this at the art opening. In fact, my relating the story to Will had been the basis of her arrest. "You told," the notes had read. Was it possible Rose had been the one to plant the clown doll with the note for me to find—twice?

"All right," Jennifer said. "Rose and I will review the contract later. For now, I'd like to see what you've got stored and make sure they are all in good shape. Some of those sculptures were pretty intricate and take a lot of care when moving them."

Amy stood, her shoulders rigid. "How can you question that?" she asked. "We're professionals. Every piece is treated with the utmost delicacy." She moved toward the door and then peered back over her shoulder. "Follow me."

Amy led us through the corridor and opened a door at the end of the hall, exposing a gaping blackness that descended into the basement. She flicked on a light at the top of the stairs and extended her hand.

There appeared to be about ten metal stairs, each step with an open grating. A chorus of oven timers went off in my head, sounding an alarm. I glanced at Jennifer. "Are you sure you want to do this?" I asked her.

Jennifer lifted her chin with resolve. "I need to let Rose know the condition of her work."

"If you insist," Amy said. "After you."

"No," I said to Amy. "You lead the way."

"I'll go first, ladies." Rick strolled toward us down the hallway. "Don't want any accidents making your way down those stairs. Just follow right behind me."

Jennifer and I hesitated again, so Amy shrugged and took the stairs with care, setting off a reverberating clank with each step. I imagined her towering spiked heels becoming wedged into the metal gratings. But somehow she maneuvered her way down the stairs without a problem.

Jennifer stooped to remove Zeus's leash. "Can't have this catching on the stairs, can we boy?"

Rick walked halfway up again and held out his hand, but I felt more comfortable gripping the iron railing as I descended the steps with Jennifer following close behind. When we reached the bottom, Zeus emitted a shrill whine from the top of the stairs and hunkered down on his front paws.

"Come on, boy," Jennifer said. "It's okay."

Zeus tested the first step, his nails clicking frantically on the grated stair. He whined again and backed up to the top where he rested his head on his paws.

Jennifer laughed. "All right. If that's the way you want it, wait for us up there."

I'd expected the room to look like any other basement with a concrete floor and block walls. But, in fact, the large space was a finished area with high ceilings, paneled walls and a ceramic tile floor. An assortment of empty display cases, shelving units and platforms lined the perimeter.

"Where is the artwork?" I asked.

"Storage is very important when it comes to art preservation," Rick said. "Especially climate control. Air can be extremely damaging. So we store all the works in a hermetically sealed room."

"Hermetically sealed?" I asked. "Liked canned goods?"

"Exactly," Amy said. "All air sucked out to prevent oxidation. We pride ourselves on keeping our artists' works as pristine as the day they were brought here."

With Rick following behind, Amy led us down a hallway where we came to another room, made entirely of metal. It reminded me of the walk-in cooler in our warehouse, but this one was much larger. One window, about a foot square, provided a view into the room. I tried to peer in, but all was dark. Amy opened a panel that resembled a fuse box and pressed a button so that the wall slid open, causing a loud whooshing sound. As the door opened, light washed over the room, which was about the size of the kitchen in Daniel's small rambler.

There in front of us were Rose's unsold items—four of her

sculptures standing in a row and six acrylic paintings separated from each other in a rack. Without the placards at the art showing that had identified each of them as part of the human life cycle, I had no idea which represented birth or which death. No life existed in this airless room.

The extreme whiteness of the walls and floor, not to mention Rose's artwork itself, gave off an antiseptic feel as if we were about to enter an operating room. In fact, Amy reached into a dispenser attached to the exterior of the room and extracted some white cotton gloves, handing a pair to each of us.

"Well, now that you're all safe and sound, I've got some work to do in my office," Rick said. "So I'll leave you in Amy's capable hands. It's pretty soundproof down here, so if you need me for anything, just press this buzzer." He indicated a button located next to the panel, then strode back the way we'd come.

Amy extended her hand as an invitation for us to enter the room. "Let's get this done. I don't have all day," she said, tapping her foot.

I touched Jennifer's arm. "Is it really necessary for you to go inside? From here, everything looks fine. And you have the list."

Jennifer turned to me. "I'd like to check for any damage before these items are released." Amy nodded toward the entrance again. "You'll want to put the gloves on first."

"Jennifer," I said. "I really don't think you should go in there."

Amy crossed her arms and released an exasperated sigh. "For Pete's sake. Can we get this over with already? I've got work to do."

"It's okay, Trudie," Jennifer said. "It will only take a few minutes."

If any of these pieces were returned to Rose with dents or scratches, we would need to know who was responsible, the museum or the movers."

She threw me a reassuring smile, and I shrugged and nodded. So she slipped on the white gloves, squared her shoulders and entered the room. She began to walk among the pieces, checking the front, back and edges of each, slowing as she felt more at ease in the room. The sculptures appeared even larger than I remembered, towering over Jennifer's petite frame.

I began to relax, checked my watch, shifted from one foot to the other, my lower back beginning to ache from standing on the hard floor.

Amy remained with her arms crossed and lips puckered in distaste. She began to pace, her heels clicking back and forth as she passed in front of me, frowning and seemingly lost in thought.

Then, without warning, she emitted a loud roar and pounced toward me, shoving me away from the door then throwing open the panel and pushing buttons. In an instant, the storage room blacked out and the door slid shut

Chapter Nineteen

I heard Jennifer shriek.

"What are you doing?" I yelled. "Open that door." I ran toward the panel, but Amy shoved me away again. I lost my balance and fell to the floor, landing on my back and hitting the back of my head on the floor with a sharp crack.

Dizziness washed over me as I heard Amy's footsteps click toward me. Looking up I saw her in double, two pairs of bright red lips spouting at me. "You bitch. You told."

"Y-you're the one." My speech slurred as I thought of the porcelain-faced clown dolls hanging in Daniel's foyer. "It was you."

"You bet it was me." Amy drew her foot back and kicked me in my ribs with one of her pointy-toed stilettos.

Pain seared through me. I groaned and rolled to my side.

Jennifer's screams were muffled as she called my name from inside the airless room. I wondered how much time she had before all the oxygen was used up. I tried to stand, but Amy kicked me again in the back. I arched against the pain, and groaned.

"You told." Amy loomed over me. "You ruined everything,

getting the cops on my ass. That boyfriend of yours was here again this morning with his sidekick and more of their incessant questions."

I turned to her. "Daniel was here today?"

"Can't get rid of those two. I'm sure they'll be back with a warrant, but I'll be out of here by then." She laughed. "I've got plans for your sweetie now that I have access to his house. You need to stop leaving your purse lying around, Trudie, where anyone can make copies of your keys."

"No," I managed to squeak out, shaking my head and regretting that I had in fact left my purse in Amy's office on my last visit.

"Oh, yes. He'll be sorry. You'll all be sorry. You ruined everything. This gallery was supposed to be mine. All mine. I got rid of the old bitch, made sure Rose got the blame. Used her pendant to kill Christine and made sure her fingerprints were everywhere. I even got them arguing about Rose's commission during the art show. Every step carefully planned and you ruined it. You told."

She balled her fists at her sides and screamed at the top of her lungs.

I wondered if Rick had left yet. Maybe he would hear her and come down to investigate. But no, he said the basement was sound-proof. And could Rick have been involved, too? Was he also part of the plot to kill Christine and take over the gallery?

Amy glared at me again.

"Wh-what about Rick? Does he know?"

"Rick? Ha, what a laugh. Christine hired him for his looks, that's all. Someone to help make more sales. Rick is clueless. Huh. I guess I may have to get rid of him, too." She shook her head. "Pity."

"Trudie," I heard Jennifer call in a voice more muted now.

I turned toward the sealed room. I had to get that door open before she suffocated.

Amy laughed. "Don't worry about her. Soon she'll be unconscious and won't feel a thing. You, on the other hand...."

She teetered over to a side wall where a large object stood covered in a drop cloth—something on wheels because she grabbed onto it and rolled it over to where I lay. Slowly easing the cloth off, she laughed again. "You're going to love this."

I gasped.

An entire row of doll clowns hung from the bar of a clothing rack. The same clowns with the porcelain faces, hands and feet. The same ones that had hung in Daniel's foyer. Each had a different expression, mirth, sadness, surprise, horror.

Amy walked along the front of the rack, swinging the dolls as she passed, their porcelain hands and feet clicking into each other. "How do you like my handiwork? Interesting stuff, don't you think? I wanted to put them on display in the museum, but Christine wouldn't agree. Said they weren't museum-quality and that I should sell them at a craft show. A craft show. The old bitch. I showed her, didn't I?"

My vision blurred again and the clowns seemed to double in number.

When Amy strolled back along the row of dolls, she stopped at one and removed something from around its neck. Something long and red. "Recognize this?" she asked as she approached and stood above me.

I focused on the object and as my vision cleared, I sucked in my breath.

In Amy's hand was a spiral pendant identical to the one that had killed Christine. Was this the duplicate that was missing when Rose invited me over to pick out a piece of her hand-made jewelry?

"Yes," she said. "You recognize it and you know what it can do."

As she walked toward me, I used my feet to inch my body back, each movement causing searing pain through my body. I reached a wall and couldn't go any further.

She ran her finger down and around the spirals of metal to the point where it pricked her skin and drew blood. "Ouch," she said with a smile. "Pretty sharp, isn't it?"

I looked to the left and the right, searching for a way out.

"Nowhere to go, is there Trudie?" The white fluorescent lighting in the room made her heavily made-up face, with its black eyeliner and rouged cheeks, resemble the clowns hanging on the rack behind her.

Amy raised the pendant slowly above her head.

I noticed movement behind her and spotted Zeus, his ears alert, his eyes on me. Zeus. I realized he was waiting for a signal. A signal from me allowing him to attack.

As Amy began to lunge toward me, I kicked my feet out to trip her and lifted my hand, pointing from Zeus to Amy, the same signal I'd seen Rose use many times. A signal that said, yes, go, do your thing.

As if he were in the agility ring flying over hurdles, Zeus propelled himself into the air and onto Amy's back. She yelled, "No," as the force knocked her forward.

With all my strength, I rolled to one side to avoid the impact, and she landed face down on the floor, just missing me.

I scooted away from Amy, waiting for her to get to her feet and attempt another attack. But all was still and quiet. I pushed myself to a sitting position and turned to look at her. One leopard stiletto heel had come off her foot. Her body lay angled, held up from the floor by the pendant, which had impaled her chest. Blood pooled along the floor toward me.

"Trudie." The muffled call came from the sealed room.

"Jennifer," I called. "I'm coming." Trying to get to my feet, my body screamed with pain, and I slipped on the blood.

Zeus danced around me, darted to the sealed room then back to me.

I managed to get onto my hands and knees and crawl to the storage room, smearing Amy's blood in my path across the floor. Pain pierced through me with every breath, every movement, but I had to get that door open.

Still on my hands and knees, I finally reached the entrance to the room. "Hold on, Jennifer. I'm here." I wiped my hands, one by one, on my clothing to dry them. Then, pressing against the wall, I planted a foot on the floor and raised myself up until I could feel the control panel. I would have to stand on both feet to get it open. Leaning into the wall again, as I raised myself to a standing position, I felt as if I were attempting to reach something on the top shelf at the grocery store.

Finally, I pried open the panel door with my fingertips. I wasn't sure which of the three buttons to press. I hadn't been watching Amy when she'd opened or closed the door. I pressed the top button, and the room lit up.

At this vantage point, I was able to peer through the small window into the room. My breath hitched. Jennifer sat on the floor against the rack of Rose's acrylic paintings, her eyes closed, her face white as her cotton gloves. I knocked on the glass. "Jennifer, I'm here. Jennifer." She didn't move or open her eyes.

Zeus whimpered and danced on his paws around me.

I pressed the center button and the door slid open with a whoosh.

"Jennifer," I said again, wavering in the doorway, wondering how I was going to get to her inside that room. "Jennifer, wake up."

Zeus scrambled over to Jennifer and began licking her ear and pawing at her until she opened her eyes and gasped in a huge breath.

She smiled drowsily at the dog and then spotted me leaning against the entrance. Her eyes widened. "Trudie. What happened to you?"

I peered down at my blood-soaked clothing and back up at Jennifer, noticing the horror on her face, laughed and then winced at the pain that shot through me. I put my hand over my rib cage and caught my breath.

I nodded to Jennifer and whispered, "I'm okay. Let's get you out of here."

Leaning against the wall again, I reached past the panel and pressed the buzzer to get Rick

.

Chapter Twenty

The trees were a patchwork quilt against the blue sky. Zeus, in his official duty, bounced alongside guests, crunching through the leaves as he escorted them around the house to the back yard where Rose was holding her first annual *Art in the Barn* show and sale.

Bales of hay, stacked in groupings along the path, held pumpkins and gourds and led the way to the barn entrance. Gordon handed the visitors steaming mugs of apple cider while Zach served Jennifer's cinnamon scones fresh from a warmer.

I recognized many of the same people from the art showing that fateful night at Christine Dugan's gallery. Even the art critic from *The Washington Post* had returned for this event. On Jennifer's urging, Rose had sent hand-designed invitations to those on the original list. Perhaps out of curiosity or maybe because this had turned out to be a glorious afternoon, they had come.

Inside the barn, Rose's sculptures were interspersed with groupings of her acrylics and some of the warmer paintings I preferred from her studio inside the house. Guests meandered through the barn, several stopping to speak to Rose or Jennifer about purchases. Occasionally, I noticed people assembled in a corner in front of Rose's metal jewelry display which highlighted, in the center, another copy of the infamous red spiral pendant. I shuddered when I spotted the duplicate of the deadly weapons that had caused the deaths of Christine and Amy. I glanced at Rose and raised my eyebrows to her. "Really?" I said.

She smiled and shrugged. "Well, it did help bring curious onlookers. I've already pre-sold three more of them."

I noticed Will and Katie entering the barn, hand-in-hand. "Hey," I said, approaching them. "It's great to see you guys."

Katie wore her jean jacket open to make room for her growing belly. "Trudie, this art show is a wonderful idea."

Will nodded his agreement. "I'm glad Rose landed on her feet." He looked away and then back at me. "Trudie, I'm sorry I didn't hear you out that first night and rushed into her arrest. I'm beginning to see that everything isn't black and white. Sometimes I need to look at the gray area."

I put my hand on his arm. "Daniel says you've got a great future ahead of you on the force. I think he's right about that."

"Did I hear you talking about me?" Daniel came up behind me, moved my hair to the side and kissed the back of my neck. Then he moved up against my back and wrapped his arms around me. "Can I borrow you for a moment?"

"Sure," I said, shrugging an apology to Katie and Will.

Daniel took my hand, led me around to the side of the barn and sat me on a haystack. Blades of straw prickled my skin through my jeans as I looked up at him, his amber eyes warm and earnest.

He started pacing back and forth in front of me. "I'd planned to do this on Thanksgiving, but that Alan Bernstein character ruined the evening for me. That's why I was so angry. I wanted that night to be perfect—for you and for me. An occasion we'd always remember. But he just egged me on until I lost control."

"Daniel, will you stand still? You're making me dizzy, and you're not making any sense."

He stopped and held out his hands. "I'm sorry."

"You planned to do what?" I asked, hoping I knew what it was. I remembered Thanksgiving night sitting in my parents' driveway in Daniel's car and me willing him to say the words I'd sensed he wanted to say.

"I wanted—I just. Oh, the hell with it." Daniel knelt in front of me and pulled something out of his pocket. He took my hand in his. "Trudie, I need you. You've filled my life with joy and color and flavor. And every time your life is endangered—" he frowned at me and shook his head, "and that happens way too often—I realize that I don't know how I would live without you."

My heart began to rise like a popover in the oven. This was our moment. Finally.

"Trudie, I love you. Will you marry me?" He opened a black velvet box to reveal a round-cut diamond encircled by a row of smaller diamonds.

I drew in my breath. "Yes," I choked out as he slipped the ring onto my finger, an exact fit.

He pulled me onto his knee and kissed me.

A brisk breeze swooped down, swirling a flurry of leaves around us, and I was glad Daniel hadn't proposed to me in his car that night because we would have missed out on this perfect moment.

"Seems like an announcement is in order," he said, standing and helping me up.

I shook my head and let go of his hand. "Not yet. I have to do something first. Be right back."

He looked bewildered as I left him and headed to where Zach was overseeing the warm scones. Zach took one look at my face and beamed at me. "Whatever it is," he said, "I want some, too."

"Zach," I held out my left hand for him to see the ring.

He lifted my hand to get a better look then grinned at me. "Trudie, congratulations," he said and hugged me. "I'm so happy for you. But why aren't you in there sharing the news with everyone?" he asked, pointing to the barn.

Tears sprung to my eyes and I sniffled. "Because you're the first one I wanted to tell. You're one of the most important people in my life."

Zeus wedged his way between us and rubbed against our legs. I reached down and pet the warm smoothness of his coat.

After all, I thought, when you've got news to share, there's nothing like a best friend.

Turn the page for recipes from
Fine Arts

Recipes provided by
Washington, D.C.
executive chef, James Turner.

Butternut Squash Soup

(Thanksgiving at the Senior Center)

Makes about 8 servings

1 butternut squash split in half (*alternate method below)
2 garlic cloves
4 sprigs fresh thyme
2 tablespoons olive or vegetable oil
1 medium onion peeled and sliced
3 carrots peeled and sliced
1/2 cup sherry
1 box of chicken stock or vegetable stock
1 pint of heavy cream
Salt and pepper

Preheat oven to 400 degrees. Place squash on a cookie sheet.

Place one peeled clove of garlic in each cavity of squash topped with thyme sprigs and brushed with a little of the oil.

Bake until soft, 45 minutes to 1 hour.

While squash is roasting, in a medium to large pot, sauté onion and carrots with the remaining oil until light brown and soft.

Add sherry to pot and cook for 5 minutes. Set aside.

When a fork can pass through the squash easily, remove from oven and let cool.

Discard thyme, scoop out squash and garlic from the skin and add to the carrots and onions.

Cover with stock. Cook for 20-30 minutes, uncovered.

Add heavy cream and purée with a blender or handheld immersion mixer. Season to taste with salt and pepper.

Return to pot to keep warm.

If you would like, add a dash of cinnamon and nutmeg.

*As an alternate method, you may use butternut squash pre-cut from the produce section of the grocery store. On a cookie sheet, mix the cubed squash with a little oil and a two peeled cloves of garlic. Top with four sprigs of fresh thyme. Roast in a 400-degree oven until squash is fork tender. Discard the thyme and add the squash and garlic to the carrots and onions.

Proceed as above.

Jennifer's Sweet Potato Biscuits

(Thanksgiving at the Senior Center)

Makes 2-3 dozen

3 cups flour
2 tablespoons baking powder
2 teaspoons salt
½ cup sugar
Pinch of cinnamon
1 cup of shortening
2-1/2 cups sweet potato, cooked and mashed (2 large sweet potatoes)
1/4 cup milk

Preheat oven to 400 degrees.

In a medium bowl add flour, baking powder, salt, sugar and cinnamon.

With a pastry blender cut in the shortening until it resembles coarse crumbs.

Add sweet potatoes and milk and mix together.

Lightly knead on a floured surface.

Roll out 1/2 inch in thickness. Cut out biscuits and place on a lightly greased cookie sheet.

Bake 10-15 minutes until light brown in color.

Mushroom and Chestnut Bread Stuffing
(Thanksgiving at the Senior Center)

Makes about 8 servings

2 tablespoons canola or olive oil
1 tablespoon chopped garlic
1 diced small onion
1 diced rib celery
1/2 pound of mushrooms destemmed and sliced (preferred mix of cremini, shitake, and oyster)
1 cup peeled roasted chestnuts, chopped (can be found ready to eat in package or frozen; if frozen, thaw before chopping)
1/2 teaspoon rubbed Sage
1 teaspoon salt
1/4 black pepper
1/4 cup sherry
4 cups cubed white bread
4 cups cubed wheat bread
1 tablespoon chopped parsley
2 eggs
1-2 cups of chicken stock (from box or can)
4 tablespoon butter

Preheat oven to 400 degrees.

Heat a medium sauté pan then add oil, onion, celery, mushrooms, garlic, salt, pepper, Sage, and chestnuts and sauté until onions are translucent.

Add sherry to deglaze pan and cook for 2-3 minutes. Set aside

In a large bowl, combine bread cubes, parsley, eggs, mushroom and chestnut mixture and 1 cup of stock and mix together.

If mixture seems dry, add more chicken stock to moisten.

Place stuffing in a lightly oiled baking dish.

Dot the top of the stuffing with 4 tablespoons of butter.

Bake uncovered for 25-35min.

If the top is getting too crispy, cover with foil and finish cooking time.

Roasted Caramelized Brussels Sprouts
(Ally's restaurant, *Savor*)

Makes 6 to 8 servings

2 lbs. Brussels sprouts washed, cut in half, bottom trimmed and outer leaves removed
1/4 cup olive oil or vegetable oil
2 tablespoons brown sugar
1/2 teaspoon salt
1/4 teaspoon black pepper

Preheat oven at 400 degrees
Line roasting pan or cookie sheet with foil.
In a bowl place Brussels sprouts with rest of ingredients, toss until well coated.
Place on lined pan/cookie sheet.
Roast in oven, giving a stir every 10-12 min for 40-50 minutes until slightly soft and desired color is reached.
Add any of the following: chopped bacon, chorizo sausage crumbles, toasted walnuts, dried cranberries, toasted pistachios, whatever your liking.

Whipped Cauliflower
(Ally's restaurant, *Savor*)

Makes about 6 servings

1 head of cauliflower cut in florets
1/2 of a Boursin cheese
1/2 teaspoon salt
Black pepper to taste

If possible, cook cauliflower in a vegetable steamer, but if not available, place florets in a pot with 2 cups of water and bring to a boil.
Cook over medium heat until soft.
Remove from heat.
Drain cauliflower into a colander or strainer.
Transfer to a food processor.
Blend on high for 1 minute, add Boursin cheese, salt and pepper.
Blend until smooth and creamy.
Adjust salt and pepper to your liking.
Serve warm.

Caprese Bloody Mary
(Ally's restaurant, *Savor*)

Makes 6 cocktails

3 cups of tomato juice (Sacramento brand recommended)
3/4 teaspoon ground black pepper
2 teaspoons old bay seafood seasoning
2 teaspoons prepared horseradish
1/2 teaspoon celery seeds
1 1/2 teaspoon Worcestershire
1 oz. lemon juice
1 oz. lime juice
1 teaspoon hot sauce (like Tabasco)
Pinch of ground cumin

Vodka of your choice
Ice

Garnish
Bar pick
Balsamic Vinegar (couple drops)
Pepperoncini
Fresh basil leaf
Prosciutto
Ciliegine (cherry size) mozzarella ball
Celery stalk with leaves

In a quart container or nonmetallic container, combine first ten ingredients and mix.
Taste and adjust seasoning to your liking.
Refrigerate overnight so flavors have a chance to meld.
When ready to use, stir mixture.
Fill a highball glass with ice.
Pour a shot of vodka (1-1/2 to 2 oz.) over the ice.
Pour in 4 oz. of the Bloody Mary mix and stir.
Add 2-3 drops of balsamic vinegar
Skewer pepperoncini, folded basil leaf, prosciutto and mozzarella.
Garnish Bloody Mary with the skewer and celery stalk.

Zeus's Favorite Dog Biscuits

Makes 2 to 4 dozen, depending on size of cookie cutter

2 cups whole wheat flour
1 tablespoon baking powder
1 cup creamy peanut butter
1 cup skim milk

Preheat oven to 375 degrees.
Lightly grease cookie sheets.
Blend flour and baking powder and set aside.
In a medium bowl, use a whisk to blend the milk into the peanut butter.
Add in the dry ingredients and mix until well blended.
Turn the dough out onto a lightly floured surface and knead until smooth.
Roll out to ¼" thickness and cut shapes with cookie cutters.
Place 2" apart on the prepared cookie sheets.
Bake for 20 minutes or until lightly browned.
Remove cookies to a wire rack to cool.

Dog biscuit recipe adapted from Allrecipes.com

Acknowledgements

I am very fortunate to be aligned with so many talented individuals in my writing critique groups, Novel Experience and White Oak Writers (WOW), as well as at Wildacres Writer's Workshop. There is nothing as valuable to me as having the support, encouragement, and mentoring of both published and aspiring writers. A big thank you also goes to my beta readers who took the time to read and make thoughtful comments on this book once it was completed.

James Turner, DC executive chef, has come through again with incredible seasonal recipes of dishes that appear in this story. It is a great pleasure to work with him as I try them out in my own kitchen and taste for myself how delicious they are. In particular, the Butternut Squash Soup recipe provided by James is hands down the best I've ever tasted and the Sweet Potato Biscuits are amazing.

I can't forget my doggie biscuit testers, Dewey, Kitten, and Mystique who all chose the dog biscuit recipe included in this book as their favorite.

I have named my dog character in this book in memory of the real life agility champion, Zeus, beloved companion of Kristen "KJ" James. Thanks to KJ and Zeus for the idea of incorporating dog agility training into this book.

Finally, all my love and thanks to my family, Stanley, Marcie, Matt, Jackson, and Steve for their support of my writing.

About the Author

Gale Deitch writes all types of fiction—novels, short stories, flash fiction and poetry. Her short fiction and poetry has been published in various literary magazines and poetry anthologies.

Although most culinary mysteries take place in small town USA locales, having been born and raised and still residing in the Washington, DC area, Gale has set the Trudie Fine Mystery Series, and much of her other writing, in her hometown, Washington, DC. Like Trudie Fine, Gale enjoys watching cooking shows on TV, reading cookbooks, cooking, and eating.

Gale works for a large nonprofit nursing home and senior living system. She has two grown children and one grandchild and lives with her husband in Rockville, Maryland.

You can follow Gale at www.gdeitchblog.com, on Facebook or Twitter.

If you've enjoyed reading Gale's books, please leave a review on Amazon.com or Goodreads.

Made in the USA
Lexington, KY
12 November 2019